"Whoa, there! Samson, heel."

The German shepherd came to a skidding halt right in front of Frederica. Then he glanced back at the man in the tuxedo giving the command, a soft whine escaping from his mouth. "Well, hello there," Freddie said, her gaze moving from the hassling dog to the out-of-breath man hurrying toward them. "May I pet him?" she asked, reaching a hand toward the waiting animal.

"Samson, what's got into you, boy?" the man said, his frown aimed at the dog while he ignored Freddie's question. Then the man gave Freddie an appreciative sweep. "Okay, in this case, I guess I understand. He never could resist a pretty woman."

"Neither could you, if memory serves me correctly," Stone said from behind the man. Then he turned to Freddie. "Frederica Hayes, meet my younger brother, Clay Dempsey."

Clay. The one Dempsey brother she hadn't met yet. And he was well worth the wait.

Books by Lenora Worth

Love Inspired

The Wedding Quilt #12
Logan's Child #26
*I'll Be Home for
    Christmas* #44
Wedding at Wildwood #53
His Brother's Wife #82
Ben's Bundle of Joy #99
The Reluctant Hero #108
One Golden Christmas #122

*When Love Came To Town #142
*Something Beautiful #169
*Lacey's Retreat #184
**The Carpenter's Wife #211
**Heart of Stone #227
**A Tender Touch #269

*In the Garden
**Sunset Island

Steeple Hill Women's Fiction

After the Storm #8

LENORA WORTH

grew up in a small Georgia town and decided in the fourth grade that she wanted to be a writer. But first, she married her high school sweetheart, then moved to Atlanta, Georgia. Taking care of their baby daughter at home while her husband worked at night, Lenora discovered the world of romance novels and knew that's what she wanted to write. And so she began.

A few years later, the family settled in Shreveport, Louisiana, where Lenora continued to write while working as a marketing assistant. After the birth of her second child, a boy, she decided to pursue her dream full-time. In 1993, Lenora's hard work and determination finally paid off with that first sale.

"I never gave up, and I believe my faith in God helped get me through the rough times when I doubted myself," Lenora says. "Each time I start a new book, I say a prayer, asking God to give me the strength and direction to put the words to paper. That's why I'm so thrilled to be a part of Steeple Hill's Love Inspired line, where I can combine my faith in God with my love of romance. It's the best combination."

A TENDER TOUCH

LENORA WORTH

Steeple
Hill®

Published by Steeple Hill Books™

STEEPLE HILL BOOKS

Steeple
Hill®

ISBN 0-373-87279-8

A TENDER TOUCH

Copyright © 2004 by Lenora H. Nazworth

www.SteepleHill.com

Printed in U.S.A.

But now, O Lord, you are our Father;
We are the clay, and You our potter:
And all we are the work of Your hand.

—*Isaiah* 64:8

To my nephews Jeremy Smith and Larry Itson,
with love

Chapter One

"Sit."

Clay Dempsey patted the big German shepherd on the head, then grinned down at him. "Good boy, Samson." Leaning close, he whispered, "We have to behave ourselves today. My brother is getting married. I'll take you out on the beach for some tug-of-war later, I promise."

Samson's ears perked up with interest, but the dog remained in a sitting position.

Clay glanced around. It was a crisp early September afternoon and they were standing in what looked like a marsh. Why Stone of all people had chosen to get married in this mosquito-infested Georgia swamp was beyond Clay's comprehension. Stone was more the country-club-wedding and extravagant-reception type. But then, his brother had changed. A lot apparently, from everything Clay had heard and seen since coming back to Sunset Island a couple of days ago. But then, everything in his own life seemed to be changing, too, Clay reasoned as he patted Samson's head and waited nervously for the wedding to begin.

Now he was about to be part of Stone's wedding to Tara Parnell. Clay was the best man and their older brother, Rock, who happened to be a minister and married to Tara's sister, Ana, was going to perform the ceremony.

"What a strange and wonderful world we live in, Samson," Clay said to the big dog sitting faithfully but alert at his feet. "I mean, here I am in a tuxedo, standing in a marsh, waiting for my brother to get married. This is the second wedding in our family this summer." First Rock and now Stone. Clay felt downright betrayed and bewildered.

He never would have believed either of his ornery brothers would get married and settle down. Especially Stone.

He stared down at Samson, wondering if the animal knew what Clay was trying to say. *Things change, life goes on.* But lately, things had been changing *too* much for Clay. Lately, he'd become restless and edgy. He needed this vacation, or at least according to his captain back at the police department in Atlanta, Clay needed some time away from the force. And both he and Samson needed some time to heal.

"I won't let you down, buddy," Clay said to the dog.

Samson did seem to understand that particular promise. He stared up at Clay with big, dark, doleful eyes, as if to say "I know you won't, partner."

Clay and Samson had been together for two years. They worked the K-9 Unit in one of Atlanta's worst areas. Searching out drugs and criminals mostly. Sometimes just search and find. Clay had seen too much death and destruction lately. And the last round had almost caused both Clay and Samson to become statistics. Nothing like a near-death experience to make a person stop and think about living. Really living.

"Hey, brother, you about ready?"

Clay turned to find Rock headed his way with a grin on his face. "Is it time?"

"It's time. And don't look so panicked. You're not the one getting hitched."

"Thank goodness." Clay relaxed, then gave Samson the signal to do the same. The dog plopped down, his big eyes looking disappointed, his big tongue hanging out. There was so much action out in that marsh, after all.

And a lot of human action around the quaint little chapel sitting by the still waters that came from the nearby Savannah River. Clay looked toward the chapel. "Is the bride ready?"

"Very ready," Rock said, slapping Clay on the back. "She's hiding out in the tent Ana set up near Josiah's house. Between the bugs, the humidity and her nerves, however, I think the bride's going to be as wilted as a thirsty water lily."

"I bet Stone won't notice," Clay replied, thinking Tara Parnell was sure a pretty woman. And his brother seemed to really love her. "Explain it to me one more time, Rock. How exactly did Stone become a human being?"

Rock laughed, his Bible in one hand as they walked toward the chapel where both family and friends were crowded into the pews, waiting. The sound of the classic and romantic "Pachelbel Canon" filled the air as several white birds, startled from their nests in the cypress trees, lifted out over the water. Clay saw the bride coming out of her tent, her eyes wide and misty, her steps almost in perfect symmetry with the flight of the beautiful, graceful birds as she lifted her full-skirted creamy satin gown off the ground. They were about to have a wedding.

The rest of the Sunset Island inhabitants were patiently waiting back at Stone's turn-of-the-century hotel, Hidden Hill, for a big reception.

Rock held a hand toward the chapel. "We can thank the good Lord and the love of a good woman for that transformation, brother. Sir Walter Scott put it best— 'For love is heaven, and heaven is love.' A man can't miss with that combination."

Clay nodded, silently thinking that he'd never been able to find that particular combination in his own love life. Maybe because he wasn't a romantic or a philosopher like his older brother, Rock, nor a shrewd, aggressive businessman like his other brother, Stone. Clay was shy and quiet-natured, but direct when need be; focused and determined, but completely dedicated to his work. And therein lay the problem with his nonexistent love life. Too many nights out with Samson, searching for the lost, searching for the hidden, searching for something or someone to bring the life back to his own soul.

"I did need a vacation," he mumbled, causing Rock to raise an eyebrow, and causing Samson to send him a low bark of agreement.

"I'm glad you're home," Rock said as they reached the aged wooden steps to the chapel. "Let's go get Stone married, so our mother can drink punch and brag."

Clay stopped on the bottom step, his eyes going wide. "Uh-oh. I'm in trouble, aren't I?"

Rock frowned. "For what?"

"Not for *what*," Clay replied. "*With* Mother. I mean, I don't stand a chance now. Both you and Stone married! That leaves me."

Rock nodded slowly, a bemused expression on his face. "Yes, I can see why you have that look of utter fear in your eyes. Here for a whole month, with Mother hearing so many wedding bells. Prepare for a big battle, brother. She'll try to fix you up with every available island girl, that's for sure."

"Great," Clay said, rolling his eyes. "Just what I needed."

* * *

"This is great," Fredrica Hayes said to Ana as she took another nibble of the wonderful bite-size crabcake centered on her plate of appetizers. "Ana, thanks for inviting me. I needed a break."

"Of course, Fredrica," Ana Dempsey said, her smile bright and cheery. "We couldn't have the whole island here for a reception without including the latest newcomer, now could we?"

"Well, I do appreciate it—and call me Freddie. That's my nickname. My dad gave it to me, and it's kind of stuck since childhood."

Ana laughed. "Sounds as if you had a parent like Eloise. You know she nicknamed all her boys after substances she uses in her art."

"So I hear," Freddie replied, glancing around. "I got my name because Daddy said Fredrica sounded so Gothic and old-fashioned. And besides, I always was a tomboy."

She didn't add that she'd always been very close to her father, and she missed him so terribly, she'd moved all the way back to Georgia just to be close to him. It would be good for both of them, since her mother had died five years ago.

"So Freddie it is," Ana said, bringing Freddie back to the present and her next crabcake. "I like it." Ana moved around the reception table, making sure there were enough appetizers left. A team of waiters under the watchful eyes of Ana's staffers, Jackie, Tina and Charlotte, kept moving back and forth from the garden to the big kitchen inside. "Even though you don't look like a tomboy at all with that long, dark hair."

"My one feminine indulgence," Freddie admitted. "But even with long hair, I somehow managed to scare all the boys away in high school."

Ana gave her an appraising look, taking in the floral sleeveless sheath Freddie had chosen for the afternoon reception. "Well, I think that's about to change. We have some eligible bachelors here on the island, and I don't think they know any fear."

"Oh, no, I'm not looking for love right now," Freddie replied, thinking she had lots of work and a six-year-old son to keep her busy. Too busy to date. "Ryan and I have to get settled here first. He started a new daycare a week ago and…we're both still adjusting. And soon, he'll be in school—first grade."

"I understand," Ana said, her expression softening. "Being a young widow isn't easy. Tara had a hard time of it until she met Stone." Then she smiled. "But it's too bad you aren't ready to leap back into the singles world. I had someone in mind already."

In spite of her unabashed attempt at matchmaking, Freddie liked Ana Dempsey. Ana had been one of the first people to welcome Freddie and her son, Ryan, to the island. They'd stopped in the tearoom for a quick lunch one day, but Ana had been so gracious and welcoming, Freddie had immediately felt an instant bond with the woman. And Tara was just as nice. She'd even offered her oldest daughter, Laurel, to help baby-sit Ryan. Then last week, Ana had invited Freddie to Tara and Stone's afternoon wedding reception in the gardens of Hidden Hill.

"Well, just keep that name handy," she told Ana now. "I might be interested once I get my life in order." Right now, she'd settle for having friends to turn to on the island. It had been so long since she'd had any close girlfriends. Ana seemed like a good choice, since she was a successful businesswoman and she was married to the preacher. Freddie had already attended church at the Sunset Island Chapel. That only confirmed she'd made the right decision by leaving Texas. This was a good, safe place for Ryan to grow up, with lots of families and a peaceful, small-town atmosphere.

Thinking she'd like to get to know Eloise and the whole family better, Freddie said, "Okay, I've met Rock, and the groom, Stone, of course. But I don't think I've been introduced to—"

Before Freddie could finish her sentence, Ana was called away by Eloise, and at about the same time, a big, intimidating German shepherd came barreling around the corner of the large mansion, headed right for Freddie. In spite of the dog's eagerness, Freddie could tell he ran with a slight limp. His form wasn't the best, but the big dog gave it all he had, at least.

"Whoa, there! Samson, heel."

The man in the tuxedo seemed amused even though his command was firm and no-nonsense.

Samson came to a skidding halt right in front of Freddie. Then he glanced back at his master, a soft whine escaping from his drooling mouth. Staring down at the lovely animal, Freddie could almost read the thoughts in the dog's eyes. *You look like you like dogs, lady.*

And she did. Very much.

"Well, hello there," Freddie said, her gaze moving from the panting dog to the out-of-breath man hurrying toward them. "May I pet him?" she asked, reaching out a hand toward the waiting animal.

"Samson, what's got into you, boy?" the man said, his frown aimed at the dog while he ignored Freddie's question. Then the man gave Freddie what she could only believe to be an appreciative sweeping gaze. "Okay, in this case, I guess I understand. He never could resist a pretty woman."

"Neither could you, if memory serves me correctly," Stone said from behind the man. Then he turned to Freddie. "Fredrica Hayes, meet my younger brother, Clay Dempsey."

Clay Dempsey. The one Dempsey brother she hadn't met yet. And well worth the wait, she decided.

Clay extended a hand, his grin sheepish. So this was the younger brother. Oh, he had such a sweet, little-boy face. And thick gold-dipped, dark-blond hair, clipped to precision. And eyes to make a woman swoon. Blue-green, and ever changing like the ocean.

"Hello," Freddie said, offering him a hand, her heart doing a little spin.

Clay took her hand and nodded, the eyes she'd been admiring opening wide. "Yes."

"Yes?" Freddie watched his face, then turned to Stone.

"What he's trying to say, is yes, you can pet the dog, I think," Stone replied, a grin splitting his handsome face.

"Yes," Clay said again, a blush coloring his tanned face to bronze. "Yes, you can pet the big brute. He's a K-9 and he's supposed to behave himself at wedding receptions."

Smiling, Freddie nodded, her dark hair falling around her face as she leaned forward to scratch Samson's thick neck. "I can see he's a canine," she said, thinking Clay must not have inherited as many brain cells as his brothers. "That does mean dog, right?"

Clay shifted in his black patent shoes. "I mean," he said, looking toward a highly amused Stone, "he's, we're, cops. K-9 Unit, downtown Atlanta."

"Oh." Freddie lifted her hand away from the dog, her smile freezing in place, his words making sense now as a trickle of disappointment settled in her stomach. Oh, well, she could still be polite, at least. "How interesting. I'm actually—"

"Hey, you two, we need more pictures," Ana called, waving to Stone and Clay.

"Oh, boy," Stone said, shrugging. "Greta Epperson is having a field day. Wants to put us in living color on the society page of the paper." Then he turned to Freddie. "It's on page three of the three pages they print, you understand."

Freddie laughed again, her hand on Samson's head. "I do understand. She interviewed me when I first came to town, what with me being the new—"

"Come on," Ana called again, interrupting as she hurried toward them, then dragged Stone back with her toward the gathering group. "You, too," she called over her shoulder to Clay.

Clay whirled around, then stopped to glance back at Freddie. "It was nice to meet you."

"Same here," Freddie said, her heart fluttering like a trapped sandpiper. "Could…could Samson sit here with me while you go pose for posterity?"

A sigh of obvious relief left his body as he walked backward a couple of steps. "That would be nice. He's had a rough time lately. He's recovering from an injury he received while on duty and well…"

"He needs some nurturing?"

He nodded, his blue-green eyes melting her with an intense look of appreciation. "Yeah, he could use some tender loving care. Just until I can get him to the local vet next week for a follow-up checkup and the rest of his therapy sessions."

Freddie watched as Clay turned and trotted toward

the group gathered for a picture, with Greta Epperson in her big-framed glasses and satin fifties-style pink dress issuing orders and posing people.

"But…I *am* the local vet," Freddie said to Samson, her smile secretive and sure as she rubbed his thick, furry neck. "I'll take care of you, Samson. I promise."

Samson's big black ears shot up, then he settled his nose against the fabric of her floral dress and smiled back.

"She's—"

"Pretty," Rock said before Clay could finish. "Is that the word you were looking for, brother?"

Clay shot a grin toward Rock. "Not exactly. I forget I'm not out on the streets of Atlanta. Have to watch my mouth and my manners."

"Please do," Ana said as they all smiled for yet another picture from the photographer Greta had dragged along to the wedding. Then Ana leaned close to Clay. "Freddie has had a rough time. Her husband was killed about a year ago—I'm not sure what happened. She has a six-year-old son named Ryan."

"Really?" Clay wanted to know more, but the photographer was jostling them around so he was forced to face forward and step out of the way.

"Really," Ana replied over her shoulder. "And she's not interested, by the way."

"Who's asking." Clay shrugged, then looked toward

where Fredrica Hayes sat patting Samson's head. The dog seemed content to keep right on sitting there while the dark-haired, dark-eyed woman scratched him between the ears.

Clay couldn't blame poor Samson. When he'd come around the corner and found her standing there, his heart had skidded to a stop just about as screeching as Samson's big feet. Even now, it was beating rather erratically. Fredrica Hayes was pretty, but there was something more. She looked very lithe and athletic, as if she worked out on a regular basis. She didn't have many curves, but what she had fit the package perfectly.

"Are you sure?" he asked Ana under his breath.

Ana's eyebrows lifted with purposeful intent. "About Freddie? Well, she said she wasn't ready for any type of relationship. She's only been on the island a couple of weeks and she's still getting adjusted…but you never know, now do you?"

"No, you never know," Clay replied. "At least she likes dogs."

"It's a start," Ana said, her expression a little too pleased. Then with a little laugh, she gave him a shove. "What are you waiting for?"

Clay wondered that himself. What was he waiting for? He'd come home to find some peace and quiet and to do some soul-searching. This was supposed to be a time to heal, not a time to fall for the first woman Samson happened to buddy up to. But then, Samson was a very smart animal. Maybe Clay should just do what he'd always done regarding his K-9 partner.

Follow his lead.

Chapter Two

The Sunset Island Animal Hospital was located just off Lady Street, the main thoroughfare through the island. The hospital was on a quaint side street that boasted tiny private cottages mixed in with boutiques and restaurants. The clinic sat at the end of the street near the bay, on a large lot away from the other houses and buildings.

Clay had walked Samson here, hoping to give the eager dog some exercise. He wasn't sure what to expect in the way of follow-up therapy. Lately, it seemed his dog was in therapy more than he'd been…after the accident.

"But we're here to get you well, fellow," Clay said to his partner. "We want to get back to work, right?"

Samson whimpered his answer, as if he understood completely what Clay was saying. Clay was about to answer him when a bicycle came whizzing by them.

A bicycle ridden by Fredrica Hayes.

Clay felt a rush of breath leaving his body as he halted Samson by tugging on his leash. "Hmm, how 'bout that, Samson. Looks as if our new friend is headed to the clinic, too."

Maybe she had a sick animal there. Maybe she'd hang around and Clay could take her to lunch later. Maybe he'd been off the dating circuit for way too long now.

A lot of maybes.

"Hi," Clay called as she turned to smile at them.

"Hello." She parked the bike beside the building then headed up the narrow stone steps to the creamy yellow clinic. "What brings you two out so early today?"

Clay watched, amused, as Samson tugged at the leash. He let the dog go, laughing when Samson headed to Freddie for an ear rub. "We're supposed to check in with the vet—get Samson started on follow-up therapy."

"Oh, right," she said, nodding as she petted the dog. "Hello there, Samson. Remember me?"

"How could he forget," Clay said before he had time to think. Then he grinned and looked out past the porch to the blue waters of the bay. A party barge glided by, the occupants laughing and talking. When would he learn to let his brain catch up with his mouth before he spoke?

"Dogs do have good memories," Freddie said, tossing her long brown braid over her shoulder as she unlocked the door. "I believe you two are my first patients of the day."

"You work here?" Clay asked, thanking the heavens for this delightful coincidence. He'd get to see her a lot if she worked for the vet.

"You could say that," Freddie replied, winking down at Samson.

Samson's big tongue fell out of his mouth.

Clay felt sure his was doing the same. She smelled even better than the gardenia bush blooming next to the porch. And she looked so natural and girl-next-door that he wondered why more men weren't lined up with their dogs. He was sure glad he was the only one so far, however.

"So…do you assist, or just work the front desk?"

"A little of both," she said, still grinning.

Clay felt as if there was a joke he'd missed, the way she kept looking at Samson. He wished that dog could talk. Maybe Samson knew something he didn't. She sure seemed to be more comfortable with his dog than with Clay.

As they entered the clean, open waiting area, Clay heard someone behind him. And then he found out the secret.

"Morning, Doc," a young tawny-haired girl said as she breezed in through the door. "I see we already have a patient this morning."

"Good morning, Kate," Freddie said, her grin deepening to reveal dimples on each side of her tanned face.

"Did she just call you Doc?" Clay asked, his gaze shifting from Freddie to the girl.

"She's the doctor," Kate said with a shrug.

"The doctor?" Clay looked back at Freddie.

She nodded and patted Samson's head again. "I see you didn't let your human friend in on our secret. Good boy."

"Oh, I get it. You told Samson this already, right?"

Freddie nodded. "We had a long talk the other day while you were busy taking pictures. But I did try to tell you, too."

Clay rubbed a hand down his face, thinking now would be a good time for the earth to swallow him up. "It was a crazy day. I didn't get to visit with many of the guests."

"I understand," Freddie replied, her smile softening. "Let's start over then." She extended her hand, all professional and very serious. "I'm animal doctor Fredrica Hayes. I took over this clinic about two weeks ago. And you can call me Freddie."

Clay took her hand, noticing her clean, clear fingernail polish and her sensible nails. Everything about her was clean and fresh and sensible. And incredibly attractive. "You sure beat old Doc Bates. And you can call me Clay."

"Oh, not Clayton? I've heard your mother call you by that name."

Clay shook his head, winced. "Never that, please."

Then because he didn't want to start stuttering, he asked, "So what happened to Dr. Bates?"

"He sold out to me and moved to Louisiana, to be near his grandchildren," Freddie explained. "I hope to improve things around here, update this place a bit—it's a lease with an option to buy, which I intend to do. But money's tight right now, so I'll have to wait awhile on that."

"It's looking better already," Clay said, again wishing he could bite his tongue before he opened his mouth. "I mean, this place could use some improvements."

Kate rolled her eyes, then moved past them. "I'll get the office cranked up and make us some coffee. Oh, and I brought croissants."

"You are an angel," Freddie told the girl. "Kate's going to school at night in Savannah. She hopes to be my partner one day."

Kate nodded, tossed her wispy hair. "But until that day, I'm the office manager."

"Nice," Clay said, his gaze moving over the clean tile floors and uncluttered benches. There was a basket in the corner, filled with animal toys. Samson immediately headed over to sniff it out.

Freddie looked at her watch. "My other assistant should be here soon. His name is Lee Fletcher."

"I remember Lee," Clay said, relieved that something was the same. "We went to school together."

"Lee is a character," Freddie said as she opened

doors and turned on lights, motioning for Clay and Samson to follow her into a small examining room down the hall. "He's a perpetual beach bum, content to work here and spend his off time out on a sailboat or jet ski."

Clay commanded Samson up onto the examining table. "Sometimes I wonder if the simple life might be the best life. Maybe Lee's got the right idea."

Freddie stood across the table at him, her big brown eyes making him think of hot chocolate and warm kisses on a moonlight beach. "That's the reason I came here," she said, her eyes darkening to a rich brown. "I wanted to raise Ryan away from the city, wanted him to have a more simple, structured life."

Clay took in that information and the way her dark eyes turned so serious and intense, then said, "I grew up here, but I couldn't wait to get away. I craved the excitement of the city."

"But you're back now."

He saw the questions in her eyes, but Clay wasn't ready to answer those questions. He didn't have the answers yet.

"Just for a vacation," he said instead. "Just to get Samson healed up and ready to go back on duty."

If they went back on duty, he thought.

"Then let's get started," Freddie said, her whole demeanor changing from friendly to professional again. But Clay thought he saw something else in her big brown eyes, some evasive quality that seemed to effectively shut her down. She rubbed Samson's furry back, then gave Clay a direct look. "Tell me exactly what happened."

"Oh, here," Clay said, shoving a large envelope toward her. "His records."

"Okay," she said, taking the envelope. "I'll read over these later. But I want you to tell me what happened."

"Why can't you just read the file?"

"I can. But I need to understand what Samson went through, how he's been since he's healed. I need to understand your relationship with him."

Clay wished Dr. Bates were here. That man would have just grunted and examined the dog. Then he would have probably handed them a list of exercises to complete. But Dr. Bates had gone west and Clay was here, staring at the lovely and determined Dr. Freddie Hayes. And he really didn't want to go into detail with her about that night.

But she was waiting.

Finally, he sighed, folded his arms across his chest and took on his police-giving-a-report tone. "It was a Code Five—"

"Use plain English."

"The narcotics agents had been on a stakeout in the area earlier that day. They tried to nab a suspect, but he'd fled into this building. They'd received a tip that he was gone, but he'd stashed some drugs there. We were instructed to watch for the suspect, and then search for illegal weapons and drugs if we didn't find him. We—Samson and I—were supposed to proceed on a search for evidence once we heard the all clear. It was an old, abandoned warehouse. We thought it was empty."

"And?"

He shrugged, dropped a hand onto Samson's back. "And we got in there to begin our search, and it wasn't empty. The suspect was there, trying either to hide or move his stash, I don't know. Samson alerted immediately, but it was too late. The suspect started shooting." He stopped, took a deep breath, tried to focus. "The DEA called for backup, but Samson and I had to hide out on some stairs. We were trapped inside with the suspect, in a shoot-out."

Her eyes widened as her skin paled to a porcelain sheen. "Oh, my." Clay watched as she protectively placed a hand on Samson's head.

Clay sank down on a cushioned bench beside the table. "Yeah, oh, my. That's what I was thinking, too, but in more graphic terms, when I had to return fire. I tried to wait for backup. I tried to retreat. But the bullets just kept coming. It was too dangerous to let Samson loose on the suspect, and I knew the boys would back me up. Anyway, I saw a chance and we took it. We headed up the stairs to what I thought was an exit door. The suspect came after us and we exchanged more gunfire. I wounded him and he dropped his weapon, but he kept coming. He fell against me and the weight of his body propelled us toward the exit door. I commanded Samson to attack then and he did. It gave me just enough time to get the suspect off me and down on the floor."

Freddie was watching him now, understanding dawning in her dark eyes. "Something else happened then, right?"

"Right." He looked down at the floor. "We wrestled back and forth. I could hear the other officers shouting. I called out, then I commanded Samson to attack again. He came at the suspect just as I rolled the man over against that old door." He looked back up at her then, his mouth dry. Swallowing, he said, "The suspect found his gun and aimed it toward me as Samson leaped at him. I saw it coming. I pushed his hand away but our combined weight broke the door just as Samson lunged for the suspect. We all went over into an old elevator shaft. There was another struggle." He stopped here, not ready to go into detail about his own wounds. "I managed to get a shot at the suspect. The suspect died and Samson suffered a broken hip." He sat silent, then breathed deep again. "That was over three months ago. He's doing pretty good—he does have a noticeable limp at times, if he's been too active. He's just not as alert and fast as he used to be. If we don't get him back into shape, he'll have to retire."

"I see."

She stood there, so quiet Clay wondered if she had a squeamish stomach. She looked pale, her wide lips drawn together. There was more to the story, but he wasn't about to tell her that part. He was here to help Samson.

"So what do we need to do now?" he finally asked.

Freddie looked up at him, her eyes going wide. "Oh, well, of course you need to exercise him." She flipped through the medical folder, then moved her hand down Samson's right front leg. "This one, right?"

Clay touched Samson on the head to steady the big dog. "You might need to muzzle him. He's still sensitive there."

Freddie whispered something in Samson's ear as she stroked his leg, then moved her fingers over his hip joint. "He seems to have healed up nicely. Some obvious signs of limping, you said?"

"Not as often now. The vet in Atlanta did a great job. And we've been through several weeks of intense therapy already. You know, the cart—that wheelchairlike thing—a leg trolley, then water therapy and the treadmill."

"We'll need to continue that," she said, her gaze moving over Samson. "He seems in good spirits."

"He's recovering slowly. But my supervisor isn't ready to release him back on to full duty yet." *Or me, either,* he thought.

"So…you brought him here to get him back in tip-top shape?"

Clay nodded, glanced out the big window off to the side. "I thought the sand and water might be good for him. We can run the beach, he can climb the dunes and bluffs. And Stone says we can use the pool at Hidden Hills so Samson can swim to improve his range of motion. We're staying out there, watching the place while Stone is away on his honeymoon."

"I'd also suggest a Swiss ball and some dancing," Freddie said with a grin aimed toward the dog.

Clay smiled, too, relaxing again. "Okay. I'll get Samson a Swiss ball and…I'll take you dancing."

"Not me," she replied, turning all business again by refusing to look at Clay. "Samson needs to dance."

"Oh." Clay hoped he wasn't blushing—he hadn't done this much foot-in-the-mouth since high school. But he pressed on, determined in spite of his stupidity. "Well, Doc, how come he gets to dance and I don't?"

"You can dance with him," she replied. "Here, I'll show you." She motioned for Samson to hop off the table, then held her hands in the air. "C'mon, boy."

At least Samson wasn't stupid. He lifted up his two front legs, his big tongue flopping in an excited grin.

"The trick is," Freddie said as she gently held Samson's paws, "to make him use his legs, to rebuild the muscles. Even though his front thigh and hip were damaged, he needs to stay strong all over. So we dance."

With that, she moved Samson around the small examining room, the dog's thick hind claws tapping on the clean linoleum floor while Freddie's sneakers squeaked in an answering rhythm. "That's it. See, that's not so bad, is it?"

Clay stood back, amazed at how relaxed his dog was with this woman. Why couldn't *he* relax like that, instead of making dumb comments?

"You're a very good dancer," Freddie told Samson. The dog glanced around at Clay, as if to say "she likes me better than she does you."

Clay could see that without the dog pointing it out.

Fredrica Hayes was a nice, accommodating veterinarian, a woman who obviously had a way with animals. She'd be great with Samson's extended therapy and healing.

But she obviously didn't like men as much as she liked animals. Or maybe it was just him, Clay reasoned.

Maybe she just didn't like him.

Which was a shame.

He could use some healing, too.

Chapter Three

"I like him, but I don't date cops."

Freddie saw the meaningful looks pass between the group of women she was having lunch with at Ana's. She wished she hadn't blurted that bit of information, but it was so nice to have other women with whom to share, she'd just relaxed her guard too much and let it slip. Living here on the island did that to a person. The whole town was laid-back and unhurried, carefree and pleasant. All the things she'd missed so much during her nine years of a hectic, chaotic marriage. A marriage that had sadly ended in tragedy and violence, because of her husband's lifestyle.

"Why don't you date cops?" Tina asked with wide-eyed interest. "I mean, yum-yum. You know, a man in uniform."

"Yeah," Charlotte added, her grin widening. "And Clay Dempsey is just adorable. In uniform, or in a tux.

Did you see him at the wedding reception? He was so sweet, looking so nervous when he made the toast. Just a cutie-pie."

Ana smiled over at her co-workers. "Don't you two have napkins to fold or something?"

"Nope," Tina said, shaking her head. "You do give us a lunch break, remember? And according to my watch, we have ten minutes left." To emphasize that point, she popped another miniature chicken-salad puff pastry into her mouth.

Jackie, Ana's capable bookkeeper and hostess, came out onto the porch where they all sat. "Just booked us another one of those romantic Saturday-night private dinners, boss. What'd I miss?"

"Freddie doesn't date cops," Tina explained, rolling her brown eyes. "Such a shame."

"Really?" Jackie sank down on one of the bistro chairs. It was midafternoon, so the tearoom was empty for now. A cool breeze ruffled the red geraniums filling several pots on the long, inviting front porch where they had gathered. "Hey, Clay Dempsey is a cop, right?"

"Right," Charlotte said, nodding. "And he's been flirting with Freddie."

"I didn't say he's been flirting," Freddie responded, wishing again she'd never brought Clay Dempsey's name into the conversation. "I was just telling Ana that he's…you know, made pointed remarks…to me."

"Suggestive remarks?"

Freddie shook her head at Ana's question. "No. He's, well, he *is* a sweetie. It's rather endearing, really. He blurts out things, then freezes in a kind of nervous, self-conscious way."

"He's interested," Charlotte confirmed with a toss of her curls. "Yup, he's sure interested, all right."

"And you know this because…?" Jackie asked, her eyebrows lifting.

"Because I went to school with Clay. We graduated from high school together. And…he never flirted with *me*. Clay was the quiet Dempsey, always trying to please everyone around him. He worked hard at school and played hard at all kinds of sports and vowed the whole time that he was leaving this island for the big city. He always wanted to be a policeman." She tapped her finger on the table. "But now he's back and he's…flirting. Clay never flirted unless he was serious. He had to get up his nerve. Yup, he's interested," she said again, her tapping picking up its tempo.

"But I'm not," Freddie said, taking a sip of her peach-mango tea to calm the jitters in her stomach. "I can't get involved with another cop."

"Old boyfriend?" Tina asked as she peeled the skin off her orange slice, then tossed the fresh wedge of fruit into her mouth.

Freddie didn't want to explain, but she felt cornered. And it was good to have female friends to confide in.

If these friends could be trusted. She knew she could trust Ana, but what about the rest?

"You can trust us," Jackie said as if she'd read Freddie's mind. "But if you don't want to tell us—"

"She does," Charlotte said, "don't you?"

"I want you to understand," Freddie replied, amused in spite of her qualms at how the women were all waiting impatiently for her to spill her worries. "But please don't spread this around. My son—"

"They won't repeat it," Ana said, her eyes narrowing in a glare that told her employees they'd better heed her gentle warning. "Right, girls?"

Three heads bobbed. "No. No way. Never."

Freddie had to smile at that. "I was married to a cop."

"Oh, Ryan's father?" Ana asked, concern in her voice.

"Yes." She glanced out toward the ocean across the narrow ribbon of road. The cobalt water beckoned her. She wished she could forget the past and enjoy the tranquility of this tiny island. But she knew it would take time. "He died in the line of duty."

All of the women became quiet then. Ana reached a hand across the table to Freddie. "That's tough. I'm so sorry. I knew you were a widow, but...well, I had no idea."

"How long?" Jackie asked.

"A little over a year ago," Freddie replied, memories

hitting at her with gale force. "We lived in Dallas. He'd been on the force there for six years. His father and his older brother are both police officers, too. They all took it pretty hard."

She didn't say how hard or that they'd made her life miserable after Gary's death.

"Wow," Tina said. "That's so sad."

Freddie couldn't tell her new friends how horrible her former life had been. She couldn't tell them that Gary had been controlling and overbearing, that he didn't allow her to have girlfriends. Or that her marriage had been on the verge of ending long before her husband got killed. "I have relatives in Georgia, not far from Savannah, so I decided to move back here. I needed a fresh start."

"Good idea," Jackie said, getting up. "Girls, I think we need to get back to work. Let's get the kitchen in order so we can knock off early this afternoon."

Ana shot her friend a thankful look. Freddie was relieved that none of the women pressed her further, but she felt as if they couldn't wait to get in the kitchen and whisper about what she'd just revealed. Soon, she was alone with Ana, the sound of seagulls cawing giving her a sense of peace. The afternoon breeze had a touch of fall in it.

Freddie lifted her head, enjoying the fresh, crisp air. "I love it here."

Ana nodded, poured them more hot tea. "This island

has that effect on people. It has a way of healing any hurts."

Freddie took a sip of tea. "I can see that. Rock and you, Stone and Tara—you all seem so happy."

Ana's smile was bittersweet. "It wasn't always that way. Rock and I had a lot of things standing between us, but we managed to work them out. I'm happy for Tara and Stone, too. Oh, and I got a postcard from them today. They're in Paris, shopping for pieces to refurbish Hidden Hill, and of course, Tara is worried about the girls."

"Your parents are with them in Savannah, right?"

"Yes, but you know how it is, being a mother. Tara can't wait to get home and help the girls get ready for school."

"Yes, I have to get Ryan settled into his new school, too," Freddie said. "I can't believe he'll be in first grade this fall, plus he has a birthday coming up in October. And speaking of that, I'd better get over to the day care and pick him up. I promised him we'd go frolicking on the beach this afternoon."

Ana looked wistful. "I can't wait to be a mother."

Freddie saw Ana's secretive smile. "Any chance that might be happening?"

"We're trying," Ana admitted. "You know, we've only been married three months, so we don't want to rush things, but we're both so ready to be parents."

"You'd be a great mother," Freddie replied, happiness for Ana pushing away her own dark memories. "And Rock—that man has such a way with children."

"Yes, he does," Ana said, her smile beaming. "Tara's girls love him so much." She went back to gathering dishes. "Anyway, we'll see."

"I hope you get your wish," Freddie said, touching a hand on Ana's arm. "Being a mother—it's like nothing else. The love you feel…well, let's just say it's going to be hard to watch Ryan grow up, but I guess that's part of the deal. Until then, though, I'm going to enjoy him being a little boy by taking him down to the beach to make sand castles."

"School starts next week. Better enjoy these last days of summer."

"I intend to," Freddie replied as she grabbed her tote bag.

"I am sorry about your husband," Ana said. "I mean, we all knew you were a widow, but I guess no one wanted to be too nosy and ask exactly how your husband had died."

"Now you know," Freddie said, hoping Ana wouldn't press for details. "I'm adjusting, though."

"That's good. It took Tara a while to accept her first husband's death. I'm so glad she found Stone."

Freddie thought about how happy and in love Stone and Tara had looked at their wedding reception, a little stab of some unspoken emotion piercing at her heart. "They make a beautiful couple."

"Freddie?"

She turned to find Ana staring at her. "Yes?"

"About Clay?"

"He's very nice and very cute. But…I can't date a cop."

"That's too bad," Ana said, a determined look on her face. "Clay is different from his brothers. Rock was once bitter and a bit controlling, and Stone had just shut down on all levels, but thankfully, they've both changed a lot lately. But Clay—he has a tender nature that hides all his hurts."

"What kind of hurts could Clay Dempsey possibly have? He seems very down-to-earth and centered to me."

Ana smiled again, then began gathering their dishes. "Like I said, he has a tender nature that hides a world of hurts. And…he was so young when the Dempseys lost their father. He might be a big help to Ryan."

"I'll keep that in mind," Freddie replied. "But I don't intend to get involved with another policeman."

"End of discussion?"

"End of discussion."

Ana didn't look convinced, Freddie thought as she walked back up the street toward Ryan's day care, the sound of the ocean's continuous waves falling into a rhythm with her footsteps. The air smelled so clean and pure, she took a deep, calming breath and put Clay Dempsey out of her mind.

But if she admitted it to herself, Freddie knew she wasn't entirely convinced of her declaration to not get involved with a policeman. Clay did seem like a nice enough person. But then, she'd only had two conversations with the man.

Clay Dempsey might be different from his brothers. But would he be any different from her husband?

"She's different from the women I've dated back in Atlanta," Clay told his mother later that day.

They were sitting in Eloise's vast, high-ceilinged kitchen. Eloise was peeling peaches for cobbler, while her trusty caretakers Cy and Neda Wilson worked on a dinner of blue crabs and fried oysters—both favorites of Clay's.

"Are you dating her?" Eloise asked, the pride and hope in her silver eyes making Clay cringe.

"No, Mother. I told you, she's Samson's doctor."

The big dog heard his name and came trotting into the kitchen, whimpering a greeting.

"Yes, he's talking about you, fellow," Eloise said, smiling down at the waiting dog. "I can't pet you right now, Samson. My hands are covered in peach juice."

Samson's big brown eyes widened, then he circled the long butcher-block work space and found a worn spot on the hardwood floors.

"Good boy," Clay said, watching the dog. Samson's

eyes held a trust and loyalty that still amazed Clay. He wished humans could be so trusting.

"You know, Samson is Josiah's first name," Eloise said, that burning hope still in her eyes. "Or is it his second name? Anyway, we call him Josiah. He lives out in the marsh—you met him at the wedding. You'll probably get to know him when Stone and Tara return from Europe. Your brother expects you to help him out in that swamp."

"That swamp is going to be their front yard," Neda reminded Eloise with a chuckle. "I still can't picture sophisticated Tara living out in the marshes."

"Tara is tougher than she looks," Eloise replied as she finished the last peach, then began layering the slices into a long glass baking dish. "And so is our Freddie, I believe. Now, Clay, tell me more about her."

"I don't know a whole lot," Clay admitted, silently laughing at the way his mother had turned the conversation back to Freddie Hayes. "She's been here a few weeks. She's living in a small cottage down by the boardwalk, not far from the animal clinic, and…she sure is prettier than old Doc Bates."

"You can say that again," Cy called from the stove. He was a big man with a precision crew cut. He'd been a cook in the navy and now he cooked for Eloise.

"I heard that," Neda said as she passed by with flour and sugar for the cobbler, her eyes twinkling. "But you're right. Fredrica is a pretty woman." She gave Clay a meaningful look.

"Is everyone on the island determined to get Freddie and me together?" Clay asked.

"Pretty much," Eloise said without a trace of guilt or coyness. "You'd make a perfect match."

"I don't even know the woman that well," Clay countered, his easygoing nature being sorely tested.

"You have lots of free time to get to know her," Eloise pointed out. "And didn't you say you'd be working with her anyway, doing Samson's therapy?"

"Twice a week," Clay replied, already looking forward to that, although he would never admit it to his mother. "We're going to do water exercises in Stone's pool and out in the ocean. And we might drive into Savannah for some hydrotherapy in the whirlpool at this big veterinarian center Freddie suggested."

"You mean, you and Freddie would both take Samson?"

"Maybe," Clay replied to his mother's question. "If she'll go with us."

"Ask her."

Clay let out a long breath. "Mother!"

"Okay, okay, I'll hush. But I was right about Ana and Tara. They're both married to your brothers now."

"Yes, I happen to have noticed that, since I attended both weddings."

"Well—"

Clay sank back in his chair, rolling his eyes. Rock and Stone *had* warned him. "Mother."

"Not another word," Eloise said, her spangled earrings shimmering as she helped Neda finish the crust for the cobbler. "Dinner will be about another half hour, Clay. You could take Samson for a walk on the beach if you want."

"Good idea," Clay said, glad to be out from under her overbearing, well-meaning analysis of his sorry love life. "C'mon, Samson," he called. The dog was immediately alert and jumped up. Clay noticed Samson wasn't as fast as he once was, but he had improved since the injury. That was something to be thankful for. "We'll be back around six."

"Everything should be ready by then," Eloise said. Then she came around the counter to touch Clay's face. "It's so good to have you home."

Clay liked his mother's hands. They were creative and graceful, just like her. He'd always tried so hard to please his mother, after they'd lost their father. He'd wanted to make her smile again. He'd failed miserably. But he remembered those hands, late at night, moving over his face when she thought he was asleep. He remembered her tender touch, even if he couldn't remember her acting like a normal mother. Unlike Rock and Stone, Clay held no resentment toward his artistic mother. Maybe because he'd been too young to see the obvious, or maybe because he *was* so young at the time, he saw what his older brothers never had. His mother had lived for their father, and then she had lived for her work. Rock and Stone had resented her for that. They'd always thought their mother had neglected them.

But Clay knew better. He knew his mother loved her three sons, even if she didn't go about showing it in the usual ways. He had always felt it in her touch. So tender, so loving.

He took her hand now and kissed it, noticing that it was veined and aged, but still soft and tender. "It's good to *be* home."

He turned to head up the long central hallway of the rambling Victorian beach house, Samson trotting eagerly behind him.

"Clay?"

He pivoted to see Eloise standing silhouetted at the end of the hall, her flowing skirts making her look as if she was from another time.

"Yes?"

"When are you going to tell me, Son?"

"Tell you what?"

"About that night, about how you got hurt that same night Samson was injured."

Clay stiffened. "There's nothing to tell. I'm over it now, Mother. I'm fine."

"I wonder," she said, one hand braced on the doorway into the kitchen.

"Don't," Clay said. Then he motioned to Samson. Together, they hurried out the front door and down the sloping yard to the dunes and the sea beyond.

As Clay followed the dog that had saved his life, he closed his eyes to the pain of his memories. He didn't want to talk about that night. And he didn't want to think about being a cop right now.

Chapter Four

She didn't want to think about cops right now. Gary Hayes was dead. He'd died a violent death, a death that still haunted Freddie each time she remembered his father coming to her door to tell her that Gary wouldn't be home that night. But then, Gary had lived a violent life, and he hadn't come home a lot of nights. But she never would have believed it could end that way, with him dying in a shoot-out with a gang of drug dealers. Gary had always seemed so strong, so sure of himself.

I'm away from that now. Away from that life.

Freddie closed her eyes and felt the rush of the ocean's balmy winds moving over her with a soothing touch, the sound of the waves crashing against the shore an endless reminder of why she'd come to Sunset Island. It was almost as if the waves were telling her to "be still, be still."

Freddie took a long breath and did just that. Then she

opened her eyes and watched as her beautiful son built a sand castle near the waves. Ryan looked so much like his father with his dark hair and olive skin, his big blue eyes so trusting, so loving. That was the difference though; that was where the similarities ended. Gary's eyes had always held a kind of cynical arrogance, as if the world owed him a favor. Her son's eyes held a mixture of hope and wonder and love. Her son loved her. She intended to live up to that love. She'd tried to live up to her husband's expectations, and now she was terrified her son would have too many expectations, and she'd fail him, too. *Not if I teach him the right way.*

I loved Gary so much, Lord. But that love hadn't been enough. Freddie had never felt as if her love was truly returned. Gary had always managed to find something wrong with her. He'd teased her about going to church, about how she was trying to raise their son to be less violent than his father and uncle and grandfather.

"You treat him like a baby, Freddie. He has to learn to be a man."

A man like his father? she wondered now. She wouldn't let that happen. And since Gary's family had treated her as if she'd been the one to pull the trigger that night, Freddie had felt compelled to get her son away from the Hayes clan back in Dallas. They hadn't liked it, had threatened her with custody battles and all sorts of dire consequences, but in the end, Ryan's grandmother, Pearl Hayes, had calmed her husband and her son down enough to make them see that Ryan belonged with his mother. Yet Freddie couldn't forget the open hostility in Pearl's eyes the last time she'd seen her. Since then, she'd been waiting and wondering if they'd try to make good on their threats.

So far, so good. No news was good news wherever the Hayes bunch was concerned.

She glanced back at Ryan. She had to shield him from the kind of violence his father had thrived on. She had to teach him to stand up for the things he believed in, without sacrificing his soul to the evils of the world, the way his father had. Gary had been a bad cop, as corrupt and conniving as the thugs he put in jail every day. She was pretty sure that's why he'd died in such a horrible way. And she was pretty sure Gary had learned it from Ned Hayes. Ned had taught his two sons to be domineering and macho. She couldn't let Ryan become that way. In her heart, she knew Ryan could be a good man, like her father, Wade Noble, if she taught him the lessons from the Bible. The same lessons her parents had taught her.

I won't let him be tempted, Lord. I'll try to teach him the right way to be a man.

She'd already taken Ryan to church here. That's how she'd met Rock and Ana. Rock had helped her so much when she'd first come to the island. Freddie intended to make sure her son had a solid foundation, a foundation built on the strength of Christ, and not the things her husband had craved and wanted.

But where is your strength? she asked herself. *When are you going to be able to trust God again?*

I'm trying, Lord. She'd brought her child here to this tiny island because it was about as far away from Dallas as she could get. She'd found the ad for the clinic while sending out résumés on the Internet and got an interview with Dr. Bates. Somehow with her father's help, she had managed to swing the loan for the down payment, then she'd signed a contract to lease the clinic with an option to buy it. After that, she'd packed up a few things and she and Ryan had driven until they'd reached the ocean. But was it far enough away? Could she ever escape the memories of her failed marriage and the bitter in-laws she'd left behind?

Could she ever escape the guilt, the nagging thought that maybe Gary's parents and brother were right? That she had somehow contributed to his death?

"I need a new life," Freddie said into the growing dusk. The wind lifted her long braid away from her shoulder. She tossed her head, about to call Ryan in for the day when she heard a distinctive running, the sound of four paws hitting wet sand, the bark of an excited dog.

Samson.

Then she saw Clay Dempsey walking up the beach toward her, his grin full of surprise, his eyes full of hope.

Freddie didn't have any hope to give him. She couldn't encourage his tender attention. She couldn't and she wouldn't. Couldn't. Wouldn't. Shouldn't.

And yet, his smile beckoned her like a warm wash of cleansing water, pure and complete and intoxicating.

Clay Dempsey was irresistible.

But Freddie refused to be tempted.

She looked mighty tempting, sitting there in her cut-off blue jean shorts and floral tank top. Freddie waved to him, but Clay could see the hesitant look in her dark eyes. Was she glad to see him? Or mad that he'd accidentally found her here on the beach?

He waved back, careful not to look too eager.

Samson, however, wasn't so subtle. The dog raced toward Freddie, his bark one of "Hello" and "You're the pretty lady who's going to help me." Then Samson looked back at Clay, as if to say "Look, dummy, it's Freddie. Hurry up, will you?"

"Mommy, a doggie!"

Clay glanced at the little boy running toward Freddie, then called out a command to Samson. He didn't think Samson would hurt the boy, but Samson still wasn't back to one hundred percent, and if the boy accidentally hit on Samson's tender spot, the dog might snap at him purely out of self-defense.

"Ryan, you know you don't pet a dog without his

owner's permission," Freddie cautioned as Ryan hurried toward Samson.

Both the boy and the dog stopped, obeying directions, both looking toward the man and woman with them, waiting for the sign to continue.

"Samson, easy," Clay told the dog. Samson held back his enthusiasm, alerted to the little boy.

"Ryan, this is Samson and his human friend, Clay," Freddie explained as her son came up to stand beside her. "Samson was hurt a few months ago, honey, so you have to be very gentle when you touch him. And you are only allowed to touch him if Clay tells you it's okay."

"All right, Mommy," the little boy said, his big blue eyes practically imploring Clay to let him pet the dog.

"It's okay," Clay said as he came up to stand beside Samson. "Samson, sit," Clay commanded. Samson sat down on his back legs, then tossed Clay an expectant glance over his left ear. "Ryan, you can pet him on the top of his head."

"Be gentle," Freddie said again, her eyes touching on Clay's face with gratitude. "Samson is a—" she stopped, gave Clay a hard look "—he's a K-9 dog."

"A police dog?" Ryan said as he gingerly laid a hand on Samson's head between the dog's ears. "My daddy was a policeman, wasn't he, Mommy?"

Clay's eyes never left Freddie's face. And he saw it all there in her reaction. Saw why she seemed so hesitant around him. "Yes, your daddy was a policeman," she said to her son, her expression still fixed and hard, while her eyes asked Clay to understand.

Ryan looked up at Clay. "My daddy went to heaven."

Surprised, Clay gave Freddie a sympathetic look, then bent down on one knee next to the boy. "I'm sorry to hear that, Ryan. Being a policeman is a hard job. Samson and I needed a break because we both got hurt at work. I'm sure your daddy was a real hero."

"Yeah, that's what Grandpa Ned used to tell me," Ryan said, his little hand still stroking Samson. The dog sat still and watched quietly. "I miss Grandpa Ned and Grandma Pearl. And Uncle Todd." He turned to his mother. "Do you think they could come visit us?"

Clay saw a cloud of fear moving through Freddie's dark eyes. "I'm not sure, baby. They live a long way from here and they both work very hard."

Ryan looked up at her through a fringe of dark bangs. "Catching bad guys?"

"Yes," she said, that same hesitant nature causing her voice to go low. "Catching bad guys." Then she ruffled Ryan's hair. "But remember, we only live a couple of hours away from your other grandfather, my daddy."

"Grandpa Wade," Ryan said, excitement causing him to almost stumble over on the sand. "We can visit him!"

Samson watched the boy intensely, but stayed in a sitting position. Freddie Hayes held her own position, not looking to budge anytime soon from her disturbing stance.

Clay stood as her hesitancy turned to hostility while the sun turned to a rich golden globe to the west, over the bay. It was painfully obvious by the way she was looking at him now why Freddie Hayes seemed so distant at times. She didn't want to become involved with another cop. Maybe because she was still mourning the one she'd loved and lost.

Clay sank back down in the sand next to Samson, and accepted that he didn't stand a chance with this woman. But that didn't stop him. Clay had always managed to take on a good challenge, just to show the world he could do it. And Freddie Hayes was definitely a challenge.

"We were just going for a quick walk before dinner," he explained, hoping she wouldn't think he was stalking her.

Freddie nodded, then sat on her knees to gather up their towels and Ryan's toys. "We need to get home ourselves. Ryan goes to day care, so I have to get him up early tomorrow."

"I start school in this many weeks," Ryan added, holding up one pudgy finger. "I'll be in first—a real grade."

Freddie frowned down at her son. "Ryan, remember what I told you—kindergarten was a real grade, too. You learned a lot there, honey."

Ryan bobbed his head. "Yeah, but Uncle Todd told me kindergarten is for babies. But I'm not a baby anymore, am I, Mommy?"

"No, sweetie, you're growing up." Freddie rubbed his thick hair off his forehead, a flash of mother's love coloring her eyes a deep brown. "Too fast."

"Not fast enough," Ryan replied, standing up. "Look, Samson. See my muscles. One day, I'm gonna have big muscles like my daddy and Uncle Todd."

The dog watched Ryan's every movement, as if mesmerized by the little boy's actions. He gave an answering low bark.

"I think he's impressed," Clay said, wondering why Freddie was still frowning. Probably because *he* was still here.

Freddie smiled then, but the smile looked forced, as if she was gritting her teeth. She finished packing up everything, but she didn't leave. Instead, she settled back on the big beach blanket to look over at Clay. At least she wasn't running away in a hurry.

Reaching out to rub Samson's furry back, she said, "Ryan, why don't you go get your sand-castle molds? And make sure you shake the sand out."

Ryan hopped up, then turned. "Can Samson come with me?"

Clay nodded. "Sure. But don't pet him. Just let him watch, okay?"

"Okay." Ryan waited for the dog, one hand held out

in a trusting gesture of age-old friendship. "C'mon, Samson."

Samson looked to his master, his eager eyes making Clay smile. "Samson, go."

Samson took off toward the ocean, barking at the incoming waves. Ryan giggled and followed, careful not to get too close to the prancing dog.

"Will they—"

"I'm watching," Clay said in response to the worry he saw in Freddie's eyes. "Samson knows his commands. He won't bother Ryan. But he'll watch over him. He's always been especially sociable around children. We used to visit a lot of the schools around our precinct."

That seemed to calm her. She looked away from her son, then back at Clay, her eyes the color of dark earth. "I guess I'm being silly and overly protective, but things have been difficult since his father died."

"I'm sorry," Clay said, meaning it. Getting killed came with the territory of being a cop, and lately, that had hit a little too close for comfort. "How are you coping?" he asked, wondering if the question was too forward. But needing to know.

"I'm hanging in there," she said with a shrug. "One day at a time and all those other platitudes."

He accepted the evasiveness in her eyes and voice. "But you don't live by platitudes, do you?"

She looked surprised, but pleased. "No. In fact, I got so tired of hearing that sort of thing after…after Gary died, that I shut myself off from the rest of the world." She shrugged again. "That was a mistake. I didn't think about what that would do to Ryan."

"Why did you move here?"

Again, he had to know.

She stared out at her child running in the surf, the big dog standing by, barking encouragement. "I had to get away…from the life we'd had. I needed to start over."

Clay nodded, glanced out at Samson. "Me, too." At her curious look, he added, "I guess that's why I came home. I usually take a vacation at the end of the summer, but this year, I asked for more time off, because I needed it. My captain agreed. Samson needed it, too. I wanted to be here at home, for some reason."

He watched her face, saw the play of emotions moving through her eyes like soft, rippling water, thought he saw a light opening up, as if she really wanted to get to know him. "Samson is healing. What about you?"

"You're direct," he responded by way of an answer.

"Well, so are you."

"Not usually," he admitted. "I kinda tend to dance my way around things—unless I feel it's important."

"I'm always direct," she replied, her grin wry and full of regret. "That got me in a lot of trouble with my husband and his overbearing family."

Clay took in that bit of information, telling himself he'd try not to be overbearing with her. "Is that why you had to get away?"

"Yes." She got up, determination masking whatever else she might have said. "We have to go."

Clay stood, brushing sand off his hands and the back of his shorts, wishing he hadn't been so direct after all. "You don't like me, do you?"

Her eyes lifted to his. "What makes you think that?"

"You just don't seem to want to be around me."

She looked down at the print of Van Gogh sunflowers on her beach bag. "It's not that, Clay—"

"You don't want to be around another cop right now?"

She looked back up at him, her eyes holding no secrets this time. "No, I don't. I hope you'll understand. I mean, I'm more than willing to help you heal Samson, but…I'm not in the market for dealing with another police officer right now. It was a tough life. I loved my husband, tried to be a good wife, but it was very hard. It's all too fresh, too raw. I'm not ready—"

"I do understand," he said, not really understanding at all, but then, he had a lot he had to work through, too. Before he could think about it, he added, "My mother will be so disappointed."

"So will Ana," she said, then she brought a hand to her mouth. "I'm sorry. Forget I said that."

Clay put a hand on her arm. "Ana? What's she got to do with this?"

"Nothing." She turned toward Ryan, calling out to the boy. "C'mon, honey, time to go home."

"Hey,". he said, pulling her back around, the soft touch of her skin making his backbone tingle. "Tell me."

Freddie tossed her braid over her shoulder, then looked over at him. "Ana is playing matchmaker."

He let out a sigh. "Well, so is my mother."

She shook her head. "We have to ignore them."

"Yeah, right. Two of the most determined women on the island think we ought to get together, and we're just going to ignore them."

"We have to," she said again, a soft plea in the words.

"Why? Why do we have to ignore them?"

"Because, I told you—"

"I know, you don't want to get involved with another cop, right?"

"Right."

"Well, what if I told you I might not be a cop much longer?"

He had her attention now. She let out a breath. "What do you mean?"

Clay ruffled a hand through his hair, then called out to Samson to come. "It's a long story, but I'm thinking of leaving the force. I'm thinking of giving up on being a police officer."

"Why would you want to do that?"

He didn't want to tell her his reasons. He hadn't even spoken the words out loud until now. But something told Clay that Freddie Hayes would understand.

"It's just…things can get so intense, you know. And that night when Samson got injured, I got hurt, too."

"You did? Oh, you didn't mention that."

"Yes," he said, seeing the fear and pain in her eyes. She was probably reliving her husband's death. "I got stabbed, but…no one in my family knows much about it, except my mother, and she thinks it was only a flesh wound."

He saw her intake of breath, saw her gaze scanning his body for signs of an injury. "I'm okay now. I'm fine. We killed the bad guy." *And I didn't want to remember that right now, either.*

"And when were you planning on telling your family the truth?"

"Never," Clay replied. "They don't need to know."

"Then why did you tell me?"

He shrugged, sent a command for Samson to sit. "Maybe…because *you* did need to know."

Chapter Five

"Why would I need to know that?" Freddie asked, completely confused by his blunt statement.

Clay tossed a stick for Samson to chase after, watching as the dog obediently brought it back to him. He tossed it again. "You've been there, Freddie. You know what a cop's life is like—"

"More than I care to remember," she interrupted, holding up a hand. "I know what my life was like, what my son's life was like. I can't put him through that again, Clay."

"Exactly," he said, his turquoise eyes holding hers. "So maybe you can understand that I've reached some sort of burnout."

Freddie nodded, compassion filling her heart. "I can understand that, yes. Gary...never reached burnout. It was more like burn through. His rage consumed him."

She stopped, careful to keep her voice low so Ryan wouldn't hear. "It made him turn ugly, very ugly."

Clay's head shot up. "Was he abusive?"

"No, no." She didn't want to speak ill of her dead husband, and she certainly didn't want Clay to get the wrong impression. "He wasn't that way toward us. But he was all man, all the time. He could never let his guard down, not even with me. He didn't trust anybody, blamed the world for all his own flaws and shortcomings. Gary could never accept blame, even when it was his fault, so he'd turn the tables and take it out on everyone around him."

"Including you?"

"Especially me." She crossed her arms, glanced out at her son. "I never could break through to him, to help him. I regret that, but Gary was a hard man. He'd seen a lot of things out there, things he didn't understand or agree with. So he gave up and gave in."

Clay's eyes widened, but he nodded his understanding. "He turned bad. It happens a lot." Then he grabbed her arm again. "I don't want to give up, Freddie. So maybe you can understand why I'm so bitter and discouraged right now, why I need some time to think about my future."

"You don't want to become that way?"

"No, I don't. I can't. One of the reasons I trained to be a K-9 officer was so I could distance myself from what I'd seen on the detectives' faces. That hardness, that resolve. Working with animals allowed me to keep my head on straight." He nodded toward Samson. "He doesn't have it in his heart to become hardened or corrupt. He only knows what he's been trained to do—search and find. I tried to keep the same perspective. But that night…something happened inside me. Not because I came close to dying, but because I killed another human being."

"It was self-defense, right?"

He looked out over the ocean. "Right. We all kinda fell into that shaft together." Then he looked back at her, the tenderness and honesty in his eyes making Freddie realize that he was a very different man from Gary. "And it just seems as if…as if I've been trying to climb out of that dark pit since then. I don't know." He shrugged, turned away. "I thought maybe you'd understand."

"I do," Freddie told him, her pulse flowing and crashing just like the evening tide. "I do now, Clay."

"But…you still don't want to be around me."

It was a statement, full of resignation and regret.

"I didn't say that," she told him, her own need for honesty casting out her doubts. "We have to work together to get Samson back into shape, and in the meantime, I don't mind being your friend. You can talk to me about anything, and I won't repeat it. That is, if you need someone to just vent to…because I do know what it's like."

He lowered his head, then cut his eyes back to hers. "I've never had a...woman friend. Girlfriends, semi-steady bad relationships, but never just a friend."

Freddie smiled, touched that he could be so up-front with her. "Let's just call it part of the package, part of Samson's therapy."

"And mine?"

"And yours," she said, wondering if she'd regret this offer. "But keep in mind, I'm trained to heal animals, not people."

Clay gave her a sweet smile then. "And maybe, to soothe the savage beast?"

"You don't look like a savage beast. More like a wounded warrior."

He touched a hand to her face then, his eyes full of dark pain. "Why is it that our wounds go deeper than just physical scars?"

Freddie didn't know how to respond to that, or to his gentleness, and she certainly wasn't ready to reveal her own hidden wounds. "You'd have to ask Rock that. He's the preacher and the philosopher."

"I'm asking you."

Freddie's heart did the crashing-tide thing again. "I don't know, except maybe we can only be wounded if we care too deeply? You seem like a good man, Clay. You cared too deeply about your job and your responsibilities and now you're suffering because of it."

He dropped his fingers from her face, the lingering

warmth of his touch causing Freddie to shiver as the damp wind of dusk hit her skin. His voice was a low growl. "Maybe I just need to rest."

Wanting to reach out to him, she said, "You know, I've never had a man as just a friend. I got married to Gary my first year of college, and I loved him, but I can't say that we were ever truly friends. I missed out on a lot of things—girlfriends, sisters, any type of close relationships. I had to concentrate on veterinary school and my husband and later, my son. It's nice to be able to talk to someone, especially someone of the opposite sex, simply for the sake of...talking."

Clay smiled then. "Yeah, it is kinda nice, I have to admit. No pressure, no agenda, just friendship."

"I think I can live with that," Freddie told him, hoping she could also live without taking this any further.

"Me, too. I guess I'll have to, right?" He helped her fold her beach blanket, his quiet intensity making her even more aware of him. "I'd better get back to dinner. My mother's trying to fatten me up."

"I'm sure she's glad to have you home."

"You and Ryan will have to come over one night," he said. "We can grill burgers and hot dogs." Then he grinned. "Friends are allowed to eat meals together, right?"

"Right." Freddie laughed, glad to know he understood the boundaries. "Maybe we can do that real soon."

"Okay, I'll see you on Tuesday then, for Samson's therapy."

"Tuesday," she said, watching as Clay and Samson started off in the other direction.

Ryan ran up to drop off his clean toys, then waved to them. "They seem nice, Mommy," Ryan said as he laughed at Samson fetching sticks and returning them so Clay could throw them again. "I like that doggie."

"Me, too, honey," Freddie told her son. "Me, too."

And she also liked Clay Dempsey.

Her new best friend.

Freddie arrived home to the ringing of the phone in the kitchen. Dropping the beach blanket and her tote on the table, she quickly picked up the receiver. "Hello?"

"It's Todd," came the harsh voice from the other end of the phone. "Let me talk to Ryan."

Freddie's heart dropped to her feet. "Todd, how did you get this number?"

"I'm a cop, remember? Now let me talk to my nephew, Freddie."

"He's…he's outside playing," Freddie said, her eyes scanning the small front yard for her son. Thankfully, Ryan was busy washing the rest of the sand off his beach toys.

"You can't keep him from us forever," Todd said. "Mama really misses that boy."

"I know Pearl wants to see Ryan," Freddie said, wondering how she was going to handle this. "And I promise to bring him for a visit later in the year. But right now, he's about to start school and we're just getting settled—"

"You moved there deliberately, didn't you? Just to get away from us."

"I moved here because I needed a fresh start, for Ryan's sake, and because I wanted to be close to my dad. Todd, I explained all of this before we left Dallas."

"I know, I know. But…we miss Gary, and now we don't even have Ryan. You just don't get it, do you?"

"I get it," Freddie said, determination making her straighten and stand firm. "But…I want you to understand that Ryan lost his father and I'm trying to help him get through that. He loves it here—"

"Just let me talk to him and hear it for myself."

Ryan came in the door then. Freddie looked at her son, torn between protecting him and letting him keep in touch with his relatives. "Okay, but just for a couple of minutes. We've had a long day and he has to eat and get to bed."

Turning to Ryan, she tried to sound pleasant. "Ryan, it's your Uncle Todd."

"Oh, boy!" Ryan rushed to take the receiver. "Hi, Uncle Todd. Yeah, I'm fine. Uh-uh, I love living near the beach, and Mom's clinic is fun. She had to nurse a sea turtle the other day. And I've seen dolphins out in the bay. And there's this lighthouse. They're working on making it pretty again, so we can't go up in it right now. Yeah, I miss you, too. I dunno, maybe one day. Mom says we need to visit Grandpa Wade first. Okay, I love you, too. Tell Grandma Pearl hi for me. And Grandpa, too."

Ryan held the phone back to Freddie. She took it, steeling herself for the assault she was sure to come.

"He sounds okay," Todd said, surprising her. "But we'd really like to see him, Freddie. I could drive over there and visit for a few days."

Freddie didn't know what to say. "Listen, Todd, this has been hard on all of us. Give Ryan some time, okay? Maybe in the spring—"

"You're stalling. You don't have any right to keep that boy away from us."

"He's my son. I have every right."

"You tried to turn him against Gary, and now you're doing the same with us."

"That's not true," Freddie said, careful to keep a smile on her face since her son was watching her with big, curious eyes. "Honey, go get washed up for dinner," she said to Ryan. After he'd gone down the hall to the bathroom, she turned back to Todd. "I have never said a bad word to Ryan about his father, and I certainly wouldn't teach him to hate his own relatives."

"Then why did you take him away?"

Pressing two fingers on the throbbing pain centered in her forehead, Freddie said, "I had to start over, Todd. You need to remember, I'm still grieving, too."

"Yeah, right. Like you cared. We're not finished, Freddie, not by a long shot."

The sound of the dial tone in her ear sent a chilling current through Freddie's body. Todd was known for his threats. And he was also known for carrying out some of those threats. What would he do to get Ryan back?

Suddenly her safe, peaceful world here on Sunset Island had turned sinister and frightening. Freddie didn't know how to begin to protect her son, but she had to do something. She closed her eyes and prayed that Todd would stay away from Ryan. She'd have to be careful and watchful, because Todd was a loose cannon. He'd already driven his own wife and children away. That divorce three years ago had been so nasty, his ex-wife had to take out a restraining order against him. He was angry about that and now the death of his brother, too. He could explode at any time and she didn't want her son to get caught up in that explosion.

"He's far away," she told herself as she made grilled-cheese sandwiches and chicken soup for dinner. "He wouldn't hurt Ryan."

She knew Todd had a soft spot for her son, but she couldn't predict what Todd would do to get to see Ryan again. Maybe he'd cool down and be reasonable if she just gave it some time.

Maybe.

But as she looked out her kitchen window toward the pink-and-orange-tinged sunset, Freddie felt a chill of fear crawling up her back. Maybe she wasn't as safe on this island as she had thought.

All the more reason to depend on her faith and her newfound friends.

Including Clay Dempsey.

That was it. She'd talk to Clay. And while Samson was continuing his therapy, she'd ask Clay to help her with some self-defense and security measures.

Just to be sure.

"He sure likes that whirlpool," Clay told Freddie the next Tuesday. They were on their way home from the veterinarian hospital in Savannah.

Freddie glanced back at the seat in Clay's truck where Samson sat looking out the window. "He's coming along, I think. The whirlpool and the hydrotherapy should help with his range of motion and keep him limber. And you're doing a great job with the stick toss and the rag pulls."

"Standard reward measures," Clay said, grinning. "Just to keep him in condition for the job."

"What if he's not allowed to return?"

She saw the doubt in Clay's eyes even before he spoke. "I don't know. I guess I'd have to get a new partner, but I'd sure hate to lose Samson. He's one of the best animals we have for sniffing out drugs and finding suspects." He shrugged, shifted gears as they headed out of the city. "Who knows, maybe we've both lost our edge."

Wanting to take his mind off that particular worry, Freddie asked, "Have you always loved animals?"

He nodded. "Yeah. I brought home more strays—cats, dogs, turtles, hermit crabs, snakes. You name it, we had it. My mom never complained, mainly because she was too busy with her work. Rock hated it—he'd have to be the one to deal with the mess and finding food for all my critters. And Stone, well, Stone was known for setting free whatever I'd bring home, just so he didn't have to put up with it."

Freddie laughed at that. "I would have thought you'd be spoiled, being the baby."

"No, not necessarily. Nobody noticed me. I kinda faded into the background, did my own thing. And I gave up clamoring for attention. It was just easier to stay quiet and observant. That way, I never got blamed for anything."

"Very smooth, and good training for your police work, I'd think. And you look so adorable—" She stopped, looked away out over the countryside. *Not so smart, Freddie.*

"What was that?" Clay teased. "I don't think I heard you right. Did you just say I'm adorable?"

She had to laugh again. "I said, you must have looked adorable, as a little boy." *And you still do, as a man.*

He kept grinning, seemingly very pleased with her blunder. "I am adorable. Yeah, um-hmm. You're thinking it right now, aren't you?"

"Okay, all right. Yes, you are an adorable-looking man, okay? I'd have to be blind not to notice that."

He looked straight ahead as they passed a big truck on the interstate. "You're not so bad yourself, Doc. Samson is in love with you."

Freddie glanced back at the dog. Samson seemed to understand perfectly what they were talking about. His ears perked up and he let out a little snarling half bark.

"In fact, he just told me to quit making the moves on you."

"Did he now? If I recall, you aren't supposed to be doing that, anyway. We're friends, pals, confidants—"

"No making the moves?"

She wagged a finger at him. "None of that."

"But if I'm adorable—"

"You are, but you're a good friend. I don't want to go messing with that." Then she turned serious. "And Clay, right now I could use a friend. I need some advice."

He glanced over at her, all traces of amusement gone from his eyes and expression. "What's up?"

"Can we stop and get a drink or something?" she asked. "If you don't mind."

"Not a bit." He watched the road until the next exit, then pulled up to a diner. Parking the truck underneath a broad moss-drenched live oak, he said, "How's this?"

"Great."

"Samson, stay," Clay told the eager dog as they got out of the truck. Samson looked disappointed, but sat still.

Leaving two windows down for Samson so the cool afternoon breeze could filter through the truck, Clay turned to the dog. "I'll bring you a treat, I promise."

Samson gave him a look that said, "You'd better" then sank down on the seat to wait.

Soon they were sitting in a red vinyl booth inside the greasy spoon. A tired-looking waitress with a bubbly smile came to take their order.

"Vanilla milkshake," Clay said, then glanced at Freddie.

"Just coffee."

"Okay, you've got me worried," Clay said, looking at her. "What's going on, Freddie?"

"I'm a capable person," she began, indecision making her wonder why she was even getting Clay involved in this. "But I need…"

"Just tell me," he said, his eyes filling with concern.

"I need you to take a look at my cottage, tell me where the weak spots are, securitywise."

He looked deflated for a minute, causing her to wonder if he'd expected something else. "Okay, sure. Why? Have you had a break-in or something?"

"No, nothing like that." She wasn't ready to tell him the real reason for her need for better security, so she fell back on the standard version. "You know, a woman and child living alone in a new place. I just haven't had time to research anything or hire anyone to look things over."

"I'll come by tomorrow, after you get off work, if that's okay?"

"That would be good. And…while you're at it, can you refresh me on some self-defense courses? I took a couple while I was in college, but it's been a while."

Again, he nodded. "Okay." Then he gave her a long unwavering look. "Are you sure there isn't something else going on?"

Freddie took a sip of her black coffee to avoid looking into Clay's eyes. She wasn't ready to tell him everything. It was so hard to talk about her fears. "No, nothing. I just want to be sure that Ryan is safe. I'm an overprotective mother, I'm afraid."

"Well, you can never be too safe."

"Right. I just need to feel secure."

Clay drank his big milkshake, his eyes on her face. She didn't think she'd fooled him, not one bit. But at least he had enough tact not to press her for more information. She was thankful for that, and for the way just looking at him, being with him, made her feel more secure already.

Don't get used to that, she told herself. He won't stay here. She knew Clay would work out his problems and be back on the force in Atlanta soon. After all, once a cop, always a cop. She couldn't count on his being around to help her or protect her. And she had to learn to deal with this particular situation on her own, since she was pretty sure Todd and the Hayes family weren't going to give up so easily.

She'd just have to be prepared. She'd just have to stay in control.

"Thanks," she told Clay as they got up to leave the diner.

"You're welcome," he said. Then he turned to her before they got back into the truck. "And Freddie, one day I want you to tell me what's really going on, just in case, okay?"

"Okay."

He didn't question her on the way home, but she could feel his eyes on her, watching her with that tender touch that seemed to draw her to him.

And already, she felt more safe and secure.

Chapter Six

"So you'd just need to call this number," Clay told Freddie the next afternoon. "My friend will get you a good system installed and he'll give you a discount."

"Because he's your friend?" Freddie asked, smiling over at him.

"That and he wants your business," Clay told her, his gaze following her around her tiny kitchen. "I told him I'd look around and give him an idea of what you need." He glanced around the long, sun-dappled room. "This is a nice little house."

She nodded and poured him a glass of lemonade. "It just needs some new locks and an alarm system."

Clay looked at the long row of windows that bordered the front of the rectangular sitting room. She had a nice view of the bay, but with all those windows, she was vulnerable here. "Do you rent?"

"For now," she said, coming out of the kitchen to hand him his drink. "I hope to maybe buy something bigger one day, but for now this does just fine for Ryan and me."

Clay sat down on a cushioned wicker couch near one of the open windows. "So this room and the kitchen here, then two bedrooms and a bath on the back?"

"Yes, and a door down the hall that leads to the back porch and the separate garage."

"One-car garage?"

"Yes, and it's open. I'll show you everything in the nickel tour, if you want."

He nodded, wondering again why she was so concerned about security. She was a widow, so it couldn't be an ex-husband. Maybe someone had threatened her?

"Do you feel safe here, on the island?"

"I did," she said, then she glanced down as if she wished she hadn't said that. "I…I just started thinking that I've never really been out on my own. My daddy is a giant man—I always felt secure with him and my mother. Then Gary was always there, throughout high school and college. Nobody messed with me with him around. He was a football player, a wrestler in high school. After we got married he went to police academy while I attended classes at the university. When his family all moved to Dallas, we just naturally followed them. I always felt safe with Gary, and he taught me to be alert and aware. I've just never had to apply any other security measures, until now."

Clay took a sip of the cool lemonade. It hit the sinking spot in his stomach, turning sour as he thought about how much she must have loved her husband. How much she must miss him now. He didn't expect to compete with that. But that knowledge, coupled with the fact that being married to a cop had left her disillusioned, only reinforced their original pact. They had to stay just friends. Nothing more.

"Well, an alarm system will help you feel safe here," he said, clearing his mind of everything but the purpose of his visit. "And if it makes you feel any better, we rarely have crime on the island. Or at least, we didn't when I was growing up here."

"That's good to hear."

He watched as she got up to move around the colorful room. She'd decorated in primary colors. Bright reds against vivid blues and green. Printed cushions scattered around the window seats, colorful throws tossed against the love seat, and a big, overstuffed bright yellow chair sitting in a perfect spot to view the bay. The room was cozy and welcoming, with toys stacked in a big green basket by the fireplace on the other wall, and an abstract painting of three birds centered over the white mantel.

"I'm going to go check on Ryan," she said, her nervous energy apparent.

"Okay." Clay stayed on the love seat, watching as she went down the short hall to Ryan's room. The boy was watching a cartoon on the small television in his room, Samson by his side. Those two had become fast friends.

And what about you and Freddie? Clay asked himself. "Yeah, we're fast friends, too," he muttered, thinking he was crazy to torture himself with trying to be a friend to a woman when he knew without a doubt he was highly attracted to her. Knew without a doubt that he wanted more. Maybe she wanted more, too, but wasn't ready to admit it. She had asked him here to check out her place, but Clay knew that Fredrica Hayes was very capable of figuring out a security system on her own, and finding someone to install it. And yet, she'd purposely asked for his help and his advice.

That worked for him. Friends did help each other out.

He took another sip of lemonade, his quiet determination steeling the impatience he felt each time he looked at Freddie Hayes.

And he liked looking at the woman. Especially today, when she was wearing a cute pair of baggy navy shorts and a sensible button-up sleeveless cotton shirt. She always wore her doctor's coat at the clinic, but Clay knew underneath that professional attire, she had a lithe, athletic build. And that long brown hair. He itched to just touch it. It looked so soft and silky, like liquid chocolate pouring around her face and down her back.

Stop thinking like that, he told himself. Getting up, he paced around the room and stopped at one of the many windows to stare out at the sunset cresting over the bay to the west, just beyond the marina. Actually, Freddie lived right around the corner from the Sunset Island Chapel, where his brother Rock preached each Sunday. Clay decided he'd have to go by Rock's carpentry shop, maybe tomorrow, pay his older brother a visit. Rock would be wondering why he hadn't seen much of Clay since Stone's wedding.

Maybe because Clay had needed some solitude, some downtime. And maybe because Clay was spending a lot of his spare time with Freddie Hayes.

She came back into the room then, her fresh soapy scent announcing her entrance. "He's drawing you a picture," she told Clay, motioning back toward Ryan's room. "It's the four of us, on the beach."

Clay grinned. "You, me, Ryan and Samson?"

"Yes." She lowered her eyes. "He's really getting attached to that dog."

"I told you Samson is good with children. He's always been gentle around them."

"You've done a good job training him."

"Had him since he was eight weeks old."

"Do you want to see the rest of the house and yard?"

"Sure."

Clay followed her down the hallway, glancing in the bedrooms and bath on both sides of the house. "More windows."

"Yes. That's one of the things I love about this house. My bedroom has a whole wall of windows and a set of

French doors that lead out to a small deck. Perfect for watching the sun set over the bay."

"Perfect for breaking and entering," Clay replied. At her wide-eyed look, he added, "Don't worry. A good alarm will sound the minute someone touches the doors or windows."

"Where you going, Mommy?" Ryan called as they passed his room.

"Out to show Clay the backyard," Freddie replied as she swung open the screen door. "Want to come?"

"Can I?"

"Sure."

Ryan hopped up, then turned to Samson. "Samson, want to go outside?"

The dog's ears went up, then he glanced up at Clay. Clay gave him a hand signal. Samson sprang up then headed out the back door, Ryan on his heels.

"Maybe I should get Ryan a dog," Freddie said, watching as Ryan threw a tennis ball for Samson to fetch. "We're just getting settled, so I haven't had time to think about pets. We had a gerbil back in Dallas, but I gave him to a neighbor."

"A dog would be good for security, too," Clay pointed out. "I could help you train him."

"I'll have to think about it," she replied, her tense expression asking the question that seemed to be hanging between them. *Aren't we getting too close?*

Not close enough for Clay, but then he knew the

rules. Even if he didn't like them. Staying friends was the wisest thing for both of them. He had obligations and so did she.

She relaxed a little as she showed him the garage, joking about her old van. That building was little more than a shed with two big windows on each side and a bougainvillea vine trailing down a trellis facing the house. The lot was devoid of heavy shrubs and trees, with a clear view down toward the bay and a scant view of the ocean past the houses on the other side. That was good. No bushes for an intruder to hide in, waiting and watching.

They moved around front again, then came back in the wide-paned front door. That could be a problem. It was easy for someone to break glass to get inside a house. But Clay would make sure he went over every detail with the company he'd suggested to her.

Ryan and Samson zoomed by, headed back to Ryan's bedroom, the dog barking playfully as he trotted down the hall.

Freddie fluffed a few pillows, then went back into the kitchen on the far side of the long, sunny room. "Samson will be in for therapy tomorrow, right?"

"Yes. He likes dancing with you better than he does with me. And I'm taking him swimming at Hidden Hill tomorrow afternoon. That dog's getting a great vacation."

"Well, hopefully, you two will be back at work soon."

"Yeah, hopefully." She sounded as if she were hopeful, too. Glad to be rid of them? Clay didn't know what else to do or say. He could advise her on the best security for her tiny cottage, then be gone. Or he could find excuses to hang around. "Oh, hey, when did you want to start the self-defense refresher?"

She shrugged. "Maybe later on in the week?"

"All right. Guess I'll be heading out then."

She looked up, surprised but uncertain. "Do you have any dinner plans?"

Clay couldn't stop the patter of his heart, but he didn't want to sound too eager. "Nah, maybe a burger at that dive down at the marina. One of my school buddies is the manager, and I promised I'd stop by one night."

He could see the hesitation in her expression. "I can't cook," she said, laughing. "But you're welcome to stay and share some of the Brunswick stew Miss McPherson brought over yesterday."

"You have some of Milly McPherson's Brunswick stew?"

She opened the refrigerator to point to a huge crockery pot. "Yes. She seems so—"

"Frightening?" Clay asked, laughing as he stared at the heavy brown pot. "She is. Taught school, like, forever and still teaches Sunday School at the chapel. My brothers and I used to be in hot water with Miss McPherson all the time. She'd call our mother and tell her exactly what was wrong with each of us, but Mother just ignored her. But then, my mother ignored most everything and everyone but her art." He drained his lemonade and put his empty glass in the sink. "Anyway, in spite of her rigid, schoolmarm ways, Miss McPherson is one of the kindest people I've ever known. And she loves to cook."

"That's good," Freddie replied, bringing the heavy pot out and onto the counter. "She does seem gentle with Ryan. He talks about her Sunday School lessons all the time."

"Oh, so you two attend church?"

"Yes." She pushed at her long braid. "Ryan needs that kind of structure in his life. I didn't give him that very much back in Dallas. Gary…my husband…never had time for church."

Clay absorbed that information, wishing he could take the pain out of her eyes. Out of her heart. "What do you think about my brother's preaching?"

"Rock? He's interesting. He doesn't talk down to us, you know. He understands the Bible and what Christ means—inside our hearts. I like that."

"And what does Christ mean, inside your heart?"

She stood very still, her eyes so dark they looked like rich brown velvet. "I'm still learning that. Right now, it means I've found some peace in my life, and hopefully, inside my soul. It also means I have to learn to handle things on my own, such as getting better security for this place."

Clay could see that she wanted that peace and that security. He could understand that concept. "You know, growing up, we had a solid foundation of faith, here on the island. Our mother was always devout, devoted, but sometimes she failed to make her boys see that devotion. It took people like Miss McPherson and Reverend Palczynski and Don Ashworth—I could go on and on— to help us. We all were taught about Christ, but in our own way, we all turned away from those teachings."

"But you're back now."

"Yes, we've all been slowly coming back, to Christ, I mean. Rock is a preacher, and happily married to a great woman. Stone's found his soul again."

"And you?"

"And me? I'm still searching, I guess."

"We're in the same boat, then. I still have questions, doubts, fear. But I'm trying. Rock says it doesn't have to be like a lightning bolt. He says sometimes faith comes gently, like a soft rain."

"It's a start."

"Yes, it is."

They stood there as the sunset washed over them. Clay could see her in the shades of gold and copper pouring through the windows behind her. Talking about faith didn't come easy for either of them, he reckoned. After all, that subject wasn't exactly something you brought up on the first date. But then, maybe it should be. Anyway, he appreciated her honesty, her need to search for a better life for her son. He appreciated everything about Freddie.

"So…will you stay?" she asked, her voice reserved, almost afraid. "I mean, Ryan and I can't possibly eat all of this by ourselves."

Clay's heart danced, while his head told him he was getting in too deep, too soon. "Yeah, I'd love a bowl of her stew. It's the best around."

"So I've been told," Freddie said, her relief clear as she turned to find bowls and spoons. "We'll heat it in the microwave, if that's okay."

"Great, just don't tell Miss McPherson. She believes in cooking the old-fashioned way—all day long."

"I won't tell if you won't," Freddie replied. "And let's not tell her that I can't boil water without something burning or exploding."

Clay took the spoon she offered him, then pulled up a cane-seated stool to wait for his stew to heat. "Well, you must be doing something right. I mean, you look healthy enough."

Better than enough. She looked great.

"Thanks. I jog as often as possible. It's easy now that I have a beach to run on."

"No kidding? I jog, too. Maybe some morning—"

"Friends can jog together, right?" she asked over the ding of the microwave. She handed him the steaming bowl of tomato-drenched stew, thick with barbecued beef, pork and spices.

He grinned, shaking his spoon at her. "Right. I think that's allowed."

"Good." She filled another, smaller bowl of the thick concoction. "Ryan, come eat dinner, honey."

Ryan came running up the hallway. "What about Samson?"

"Samson, c'mon boy," Clay called, watching as the dog came trotting faithfully up the hallway. "Samson, sit," Clay said, his tone gentle. The dog plopped onto its hind legs, watching Ryan's every move. "I'll feed you later, boy, I promise."

"I have some dog food around here somewhere," Freddie said, hopping up to go into a small storage room off the kitchen. "Sometimes I bring patients home overnight."

"Thanks," Clay said, admiring the way she seemed so organized and thorough in her work. And caring. He liked that about her.

Soon, Samson was smacking his lips to Dog Chow while the humans enjoyed the meaty, spicy taste of Miss McPherson's famous Brunswick stew.

"This is nice," Clay remarked after his third bowl.

"Yes." Freddie's smile was radiant and sure. "The stew is delicious."

"When can I see Uncle Todd?" Ryan asked out of the blue as he shoveled in mouthfuls.

Freddie's smile died on her lips. She dropped her spoon into her bowl, her eyes darting toward her son.

"I don't know, honey. It's hard since we don't live near him anymore."

"He could come and visit," Ryan said, completely unaware of the sudden tension falling like lightning through the room. "Could he, Mommy?"

"Maybe." Freddie took her unfinished stew to the sink.

"Who's Uncle Todd?" Clay asked, his tone casual while he watched Freddie for a reaction.

"My dad's older brother," Ryan said through a bite of cracker. "He misses me."

"I'm sure he does," Clay replied. "I'd better get my dirty dishes over to the sink," he told the boy as he got up and went to stand by Freddie. In a low voice, he said, "I take it you have concerns about Uncle Todd?"

She didn't look up, just kept washing at the already clean bowl in her hand. "It's complicated. He…he's not over Gary's death. He just wants to see Ryan."

"And?"

She turned to look at him then, her eyes a blank wall of intense brown. "And…I told Ryan we might visit Gary's family later on around the holidays."

Clay didn't press her on this, since it was really none of his business. But his gut told him something wasn't right here. Why would Freddie go from bubbly and content to wary and downright frightened at just the mention of Todd's name? Clay had a feeling he knew the answer to that question, and he figured that was the reason Freddie had asked for his help with security.

Was Todd Hayes threatening Freddie?

Clay looked around the bright, clean cottage and suddenly saw it as more than a cute house near the bay. It was a cute house with too many windows and doors. A place where an intruder could easily break in and take whatever he wanted.

Even a little boy.

Chapter Seven

"So what brings you by?"

Clay stood in the doorway of Rock's workshop, taking in the scent of wood shavings and sawdust mixed with the fresh crisp smell of the sea breeze coming in through the thrown-open doors on both sides. "Oh, Samson and I went for an early morning jog on the beach. Just saw the doors open and thought I'd see what my big brother's been up to lately. Besides enjoying his bride, of course."

Rock stopped working on the drawing he had propped on his design table, a smile plastered on his face like varnish to veneer. "I have been enjoying my new bride, that's a fact, brother. Life is good. Really good. And it's nice to have a visit from you. I've been meaning to talk to you."

"About what?" Clay asked as he pushed off the door and came into the cluttered workshop. Samson lay just outside the door, ever watchful.

"Oh, about this and that," Rock said as he reached into a small refrigerator and tossed Clay a soda. Popping the top on his own, he took a long sip. "Mother is worried about you."

Clay shrugged, ruffled his thick, clipped hair. "Nothing to worry about. I'm fine."

Rock eyed him much in the same way he used to when they were growing up. "I don't believe you."

Not liking the shift in this conversation, Clay picked up a wood shaver. "Believe what you want. *I'm* the happy-go-lucky Dempsey, remember?"

Rock nodded, took another swallow of his drink. "I do remember. I also remember that you kept things inside, behind that content smile. Look, we just want to know the whole story, about that night."

Clay didn't want to talk about that night. At all. He glanced out at Samson, tipped his drink can toward the dog. "My partner was hurt in the line of duty and now he's here to heal up so we can get back to work."

Rock stared at the dog. Samson stared back, still panting from the long run. "I know you care about Samson, but what about you? I mean, why the extended vacation?"

"Already tired of having me around?"

Rock pushed at the open door of a broken cabinet sitting in the corner. "No. We're very glad you're here. But you never come home for more than a week at a time and now you're here for a month. C'mon, Clay. You're usually champing at the bit to get back to work."

"I needed some downtime," Clay said, careful to avert his gaze from his brother's knowing eyes. He looked out toward the bay. From this spot, he could see the lighthouse that sat on a jutting spot of land at the tip of the island. "How's the restoration project coming?" he asked, indicating the gleaming white structure with a nod of his head.

"The lighthouse is just about finished," Rock said, his eyes still on Clay. "But our conversation is not, so stop trying to change the subject. What's up, little brother?"

Clay wished Rock wasn't so intuitive. "Nothing is up. Can't a man come home for a visit?"

Rock held up a hand. "As I said, we're all glad to have you back, but…we also want you to know we're here to help, if you need us."

"I don't," Clay said, folding his arms across his chest in a stance of resistance. "I just need some peace and quiet. Hint. Hint."

"Fair enough." Rock finished his drink and tossed the can in a container marked Recycle. "Look, Clay, being a police officer isn't easy. And we've heard you were hurt in some way that night, too. But we need details. Mother especially needs to know that you're healed up, too."

Clay shrugged. A flash of his mother's soft hand on his forehead floated through his mind like a slow-sailing boat. Clay stubbornly pushed that image away. He wouldn't give Rock the satisfaction. "Funny, she never worried much about my scrapes and bruises when we were growing up."

"That's not fair," Rock replied, a hand on his design table as he leaned forward. "She's trying to make amends for that, in case you haven't noticed."

"Yes, I've noticed, and no, I'm not being fair. But I feel a bit on the defensive here. She's found proper mates for both you and Stone. Now she thinks it's my turn. I'll tell Mother she doesn't have to worry about me. I'm all healed up and I'm not looking for love."

"Okay, but word is that you've been seen around town with Freddie Hayes a lot. Mother is pleased as punch about that, at least. So be forewarned. She might not have hovered over us when we were little, but she's definitely in a mothering mode now. And that means she's highly into matchmaking and healing all wounds, including the childhood ones."

Clay leaned both hands on Rock's worktable, then gave his brother a serious glare. "Freddie is treating Samson. *My dog*. He's still going through therapy. I'm *not*. So I don't need anyone hovering over me, okay?" When Rock only stared at him with doubting eyes, he tossed his empty can into the bin and lifted his eyebrow. "Hello?"

"I hear you. Tell that to our mother."

"I will. And I'll also tell her to stay out of my business. You know, I've never held any bitterness toward

Mother the way you and Stone have. But now I'm beginning to develop some big-time resentment."

"Maybe it was there inside you all along," Rock replied. "Life is the art of being well deceived, according to William Hazlitt."

"I don't know William what's-his-name," Clay retorted, a raw anger coloring the words. "And I don't have a problem with our mother. At least, I didn't until now."

"Think about it," Rock said, his tone gentle. "You're deceiving yourself if you don't harbor some sort of resentment, Clay. Stone and I were honest with our feelings—that's about the only thing we were truly honest about."

Clay shrugged, held his hands out, palms up. "Well, I've always been honest about *everything,* so there you have it. No hidden agendas, no secret bitterness."

"But are you happy?"

"Is this one of your sermons?"

"No, just a brother talking to a brother."

"Look, I only came by for a visit, not a let's-see-if-we-can-figure-out-Clay's-problem talk."

"Well, I'm glad you came by," Rock said. "I needed an excuse to quit working on this bathroom-cabinet design. I'm still trying to iron out the details and I've stalled out. It's for one of the many bathrooms at Hidden Hill, so it can wait. I'm sure Stone isn't thinking about cabinets right now, wherever he is."

That made Clay smile. "The lucky bridegroom, off

on his European honeymoon with a gorgeous, smart blonde. Stone always did get the best-looking women."

"Yeah, but they usually ended up mad at him and hating him for life."

"Let's hope Tara hangs in there."

"Oh, I think this one's a keeper," Rock said, clearly relaxing now that they had changed the subject. Then he came around the worktable and slapped Clay on the back. "Let's go fishing."

"Fishing? What, so you can get me out in a boat and have a captive audience?"

"No, so we can just visit and have some fun." Rock quirked a dark eyebrow. "When was the last time you had fun, anyway, little brother?"

Clay saw by his brother's sincere expression that Rock was trying to back off. He also knew his brother was only trying to help him. "Fun? I remember fun. Sure, I might be up to some fishing. But no philosophy, okay?"

Rock grinned. "Why doesn't anyone appreciate my propensity to intersperse a bit of wisdom into my conversations?"

"Maybe because you're so good at it, we just get plain tired of it? Or maybe because you're so bad at it, and so obvious, we just want to throw you in the bay."

Rock slapped a hand to his heart in mock pain, then quoted Horace, "'Ah, the irritable tribe of poets.'" Then he grinned. "Could be. Well, at least Ana appreciates my wisdom."

"That and your handsome mug, right?"

"Right." Rock started closing up shop. "Now, brother, are you ready to fish with a real pro?"

"Oh, you know one?"

"Very funny."

Clay watched as Rock straightened his saws and routers. He had to admire his brother's talent. Rock was an artist when it came to carpentry work. Beautifully detailed armoires, dressers, tables and cabinets stood around the long workshop, some of them antique and refurbished, some of them handmade by Rock.

Clay watched as Rock made sure all the saws were shut down and each tool was replaced into its proper place. "Fishers of men, that's what Daddy used to tell us to be, remember?"

"I remember," Rock said, stopping to look at Clay. "He wanted his sons to be more than just good fishermen. He wanted us to be decent, faith-filled human beings."

Clay stopped just outside and waited as Rock locked up the big barn doors on his workshop. "I thought I was being that, Rock. I truly did."

Rock turned to stare at him, all humor gone from his blue eyes. "Clay, you know you can tell me anything and it won't go any further."

Clay looked up at a moss-encased live oak, saw the sun's rays filtering down through the great century-old tree like a light from the clouds. "Maybe once we're out on that boat."

"Okay." Rock put a hand on his back. "It is good to have you home, whatever your reasons. And I hope things between you and Freddie—"

"We're just friends."

"'Friendship is a single soul dwelling in two bodies,'" Rock said. At Clay's groan of protest, he shrugged. "Hey, it's Aristotle, what can I say?"

Clay gave Samson a command and the dog hopped up to follow them, eager to be out on another adventure. "Just say you won't quote anybody else, please, or I might have to give you a quote of my own, after I toss you overboard, that is."

"Oh, and what's that?"

"Don't rock the boat."

They both laughed as they headed to Rock's old beat-up utility van so they could drive the short distance to the marina where Rock kept a small speedboat docked. The morning was still and unmoving, like a painted picture of a quiet, tranquil bay on some faraway island. But deep down inside, Clay felt as if his whole world had shifted. He'd never planned on coming home only to hear his brother accuse him of harboring harsh feelings toward their mother.

And he'd never dreamed of coming home to find the perfect woman, only to realize he could never have that woman.

It looked as if he was the one rocking the boat.

"We found him over there amongst the rocks in Eloise's sculpture garden. We figured you'd know what to do, Freddie."

Freddie nodded at Cy Wilson's explanation for calling her to Eloise's house just when she'd stopped for an early lunch at the office. Then she hugged the orange-and-gold-colored stray kitten close, trying to give warmth to the tiny creature as she examined his scrawny body. "I think his foot is either badly bruised or broken. Poor baby. He must have gotten it wedged in between one of the rocks. No wonder you heard him crying out."

Eloise's usually serene face crinkled in concern. "Can you fix him, Freddie?"

"I think so," Freddie said. "I'll need to take him back to the clinic, of course, and set his little foot."

"Can we do anything to help?" Neda asked, her hands on her apron as she looked at the fluffy ball of fur in Freddie's arms.

"I'll need a container of some sort—a box or a cage—to get him to the clinic."

"That's why we called you, dear," Eloise said. "We didn't want to hurt him by trying to get him there ourselves." She glanced around the massive yard. "Someone must have abandoned the poor thing. At least he found his way here. He needs some special treatment."

"I'll take care of him," Freddie assured them. "I think he's going to be just fine once we check him out and fix him up."

"And feed him," Cy said, grinning. "Little fellow looks half-starved. I'll go find a sturdy box for you."

"Thanks," Freddie said, still stroking the kitten's soft, downy head. "It's okay, baby. It's going to be okay."

She wished she could convince herself of that. Todd had called again last night, and reluctantly, she'd let him talk to Ryan. Now Ryan was more gung ho than ever to either go back to Texas to visit Uncle Todd or have the man come to Sunset Island to visit them. She didn't know how to explain to her son that they couldn't do either right now. For more reasons than one.

Todd Hayes was a volatile, angry man. She didn't want Ryan witnessing that type of personality again, not so soon after she'd dragged him across the country to start a new life.

Worried, Freddie kept stroking the kitten until she felt a hand on her arm and looked up to find Eloise staring at her. "Freddie, are you all right?"

"Oh, fine," Freddie replied. "I just hate to see an animal hurt."

"Then you're in the right profession," Eloise replied. "Why don't we sit down until Cy comes back with that box."

Freddie sank down into one of the cushiony chairs scattered around Eloise's inviting garden. "It's so lovely here," she said, enjoying the scent of roses and jasmine. She could hear the bees buzzing hungrily at the last blossoms of summer. It brought her some measure of peace, at least.

"I love my garden," Eloise replied, her silver eyes still centered on Freddie. "And how are you liking it here, on the island?"

"I love it here," Freddie said, meaning it. "Ryan and I couldn't be better."

"That's good." At a dog's excited bark, Eloise lifted her head to stare off into the distance. "Oh, looks as if we have company."

Freddie glanced back, hearing voices right along with that now-familiar bark. And saw Rock and Clay coming up the shell-covered path, Samson nipping at their heels.

"I caught that big one," Rock was saying, a mischievous grin on his face.

"Now, now, brother, if I remember correctly, I caught the big one. Remember, you almost fell out of the boat helping me reel him in."

Eloise rose to smile at her sons. "I think both of you are full of baloney and probably coming to find some lunch, since I don't see any fish."

"We left them in the van," Rock explained, sheepish. Then he glanced at Freddie. "Hello, Doc."

Freddie nodded at Rock, then looked up at Clay. He looked surprised, but pleased to find her sitting in his mother's garden.

"Hello," she said, trying to tamp down her erratic emotions. He looked good in his jogging shorts and muscle shirt, with a day's growth of beard on his tanned face. Too good.

"Hi," Clay said, his glance moving over her, his azure eyes washing her with a warm touch. "What brings you here?"

"This," she said, getting up to show him the kitten. "My latest patient."

Clay immediately came over to pet the little cat. "So you make house calls?"

"Yes, I do."

"That's nice." His expression indicated she could call at his house anytime.

Freddie just stood there, letting him stroke the cat while she pushed back images and sensations of what it would be like to have his hands touching her face.

Samson came barreling up, sniffing and barking his protest as he glared at the little cat with overly zealous brown eyes.

The kitten immediately unsheathed its claws and hissed, only to meow in pain as it tried to squirm out of Freddie's arms.

"Samson, sit!" Clay said, rolling his eyes. "This is not your lunch, buddy."

"He wouldn't mind it," Eloise said, laughing at the dog. "Samson, come see me."

"Go," Clay said, then after making sure Samson was on the other side of the brick patio, he turned back to Freddie. "Going to take him in?"

"Yes. His right front leg is hurt. It's either sprained or broken."

"Need some help?"

She shook her head, acutely aware that Rock and Eloise and even Neda, were all silently watching them. "I think I can manage. Cy went to find a container."

Rock broke the silence. "Mother, we did come hoping for some lunch." He winked and smiled at Neda. "What's on the menu today?"

Neda chuckled. "Virginia baked-ham sandwiches with fresh tomatoes from Cy's garden and Vidalia onions, delivered straight from Vidalia, Georgia."

"To die for," Rock said, holding his stomach. "Our fish aren't that impressive."

"Oh, and apple crumb cake for dessert," Neda said, a smug smile on her lips. "Shall I sit three extra places?"

"Freddie, can you stay?" Eloise asked, a hopeful gleam in her eyes.

"No, I have to get this little one back to the clinic," Freddie said. "But thanks for offering."

Cy came down the lane then, holding a cardboard box just big enough to carry the kitten. Clay held the box so Freddie could put the tiny animal inside, his steady, quiet gaze touching on Freddie again.

"Two places then," Eloise said to Neda. "What an exciting morning. A hurt animal in my garden and lunch with two of my sons."

"Make that one, Mother," Clay said, surprising everyone. "I'm going to go with Freddie, help hold this critter in his box."

"Oh, all right," Eloise said, then she glanced at Freddie with a shrug. "Clay always did have a deep heart for animals—not that I always approved the pets he'd bring home. Snakes and lizards aren't my favorite housemates."

Rock nodded. "My brother never could turn away a stray."

Freddie looked over at Clay, her heart pounding with a mixture of pleasure and dread because his eyes went a soft, deep shade of azure. Did Clay consider her a stray? Someone who needed some tender loving care? Someone who'd become washed-out and had now washed up on this beach, looking for a new life? Or was he the stray this time?

"You don't have to come with me," she said, her words and her stance stubborn and defensive. "After all, I do this for a living."

"I know that," he said as he held the box steady while the meowing kitten tried to climb out. "But friends can help friends, right?"

Aware that everyone was staring, she nodded. "Sure. Of course. And what about Samson?"

"He can ride in the back seat—and he will behave."

"Okay," she said, her voice as uncertain and shaky as the meowing kitten's cries. Then she gave Eloise a grateful look. "Thanks for calling me. I'll take care of him, I promise."

Eloise looked over at Clay then back to Freddie,

her expression full of questions regarding which one of them Freddie was referring to, the kitten or her son?

Freddie couldn't give Eloise Dempsey any reassurances or hope regarding Clay. She didn't know the answer to that herself.

But she did know that seeing Clay again and being near him made her feel the same way this poor kitten must be feeling right about now. Safe but unsure. Secure but confused. Comforted but cornered. The kitten, as hurt and scared as it was, still wanted out of the box. Wanted its freedom, in spite of the risks.

So did Freddie. She was determined to get away from the strong emotions brewing inside her every time she saw Clay Dempsey.

Because she could never be boxed in by a policeman's rules again.

Chapter Eight

"He sure wants out of this box."

Clay stood holding the squirming kitten while Freddie got the examining table ready. She'd been quiet on the short ride to the clinic, then she'd gone into her professional mode the minute they'd hit the doors to the waiting room.

"Kate, where's Lee? I need him immediately. We've got a tiny patient with a possible fracture."

"Got it, boss," Kate called out as she hurried down the sterile hallway toward the room in back where they kept animals overnight. "Hey, Lee, Dr. Freddie needs you."

"Right there," a grainy voice called from the back of the clinic.

Clay stood just inside the door of the examining room. Finally giving up on the box, he carefully took the pawing kitten out and held him to his chest, then glanced back into the waiting room to make sure Samson was okay.

Samson gave him a look that said "What about me?" then shot the offending kitten a glare as he reluctantly sank down to watch and wait.

"Bring him over here," Freddie said to Clay, her eyes on the kitten. Which allowed her to avoid looking at Clay.

Maybe he shouldn't have been so helpful, Clay thought as he handed her the cat. Maybe he should have stayed and had a big ham sandwich and some of that crumb cake instead. He looked at Freddie, watched as her long brown braid slipped over her shoulder, and decided crumb cake could wait.

Knowing his train of thought was taking a dangerous turn, Clay glanced up when Lee Fletcher walked into the room. "Hey, Lee."

"Clay Dempsey! How are you, man?"

"I'm good." Clay shook Lee's hand, grinning at Lee's laid-back attitude and attire. He had on a Life's A Beach T-shirt that had obviously seen better days and a pair of faded shorts that had probably once been olive drab. He wore flip-flops and his hair, gray-tinged and long, was pulled back into a haphazard ponytail.

"Well, well," Lee said, helping Freddie hold down the kitten, "we got us a live one here, don't we, Doc?"

"Yes, we do," Freddie said as she quickly worked her

way over the kitten's body. "Hold him steady while I check his hurt leg, Lee."

Lee turned serious, holding the cat with a firm but gentle grip while Freddie went about her work. "Where'd y'all find him?"

"Eloise's house," Freddie answered, shooting a glance at Clay just long enough to make him feel as if he were in the way.

Taking the hint, he said, "I'll just wait outside with Samson."

"You don't have to do that," Freddie said, her eyes on the kitten. "We can take it from here."

"I don't mind."

"Suit yourself."

Clay decided he would do just that. He *would* suit himself. And what *himself* wanted to do right now was have a long talk with Dr. Freddie Hayes. She seemed as put out with him as a bumblebee being chased by a baseball bat. He was a patient man. He could wait her out, all day if need be.

An hour later, Freddie came out into the waiting room, glanced around to make sure there were no more patients, then found Clay sitting in a corner reading a veterinary magazine. "You're still here."

"Still here," he said, giving the words a special emphasis that dragged across her tired nerve endings like seaweed hitting a snag. "How's the patient?"

"He's comfortable for now. His leg is badly bruised, but not broken. We wrapped it, so he should be good as new in a few days."

She sank down onto the long covered bench. "Thank goodness it's been a slow day around here. I forgot to eat lunch."

Clay dropped the magazine and stood up. "C'mon."

"What?" Freddie didn't have time to avoid his hand pulling her right back up.

"What you need is a Two-Mike cheeseburger."

Freddie frowned and tried to pull away. "What I need is to go get Ryan and go home and take a nice bubble bath." She immediately regretted saying that after she saw the flare of interest in Clay's eyes. "Oh, never mind."

He held her with a firm grip on one wrist. "Never mind what? Never mind that I want to take you to lunch? Never mind that I like spending time with you? Never mind that I'm attracted to you?"

"Yes, never mind all of that." She hated being so cranky, but then skipping lunch and worrying about dysfunctional in-laws had that effect on a person.

"What did I do to set you off?"

She looked up at him, saw the hurt and disappointment in his eyes. "You didn't do anything, Clay. It's me. I'm the one with the problem."

"Because of me? Because I came back here with you today?"

She nodded, felt like crying. "That and…because… well, you're so *nice*."

Clay frowned right along with her. "Nice? I'm too nice? Well, that really gives a fellow a lot of confidence. What's so wrong with nice, anyway?"

She managed to pull away before the lack of food and her threatening headache caused her to fall apart. "I'm not used to nice."

The silence stretched between them like an endless shoreline, long and glaringly white.

Then she felt it, a soft, tender touch on her arm. Clay turned her to face him, then brought his hand up to her cheek. His fingers felt like a sweet wind moving over her skin. "Well, get used to it," he said.

And then, he did something that caused all of her resolve and her resentment to melt and fall away like water pouring out over a bed of rocks. He pulled her into his arms and held her with a tight gentleness that left her speechless and drained. He didn't squeeze her; he didn't push at her; he didn't demand anything from her. He just held her.

It was her undoing. She savored the unfamiliar feeling of being held in such a gentle, sure way. She willed herself to relax and enjoy the moment, just for this moment. She told herself that even though Clay had been molded and shaped by being a cop, the man behind the uniform was a very different man from her husband. Clay was a good man, a good officer of the law. Maybe she had misjudged him.

She finally pulled away, then looked up into his eyes. "What's a Two-Mike cheeseburger, anyway?"

He smiled then, his eyes crinkling, his chin jutting out in a triumphant defiance. "Only the best burger this side of Savannah."

"Sounds wonderful," she said, giving in to the need to be with him. "I have about a half hour before I have to pick up Ryan. Might as well take him with us. If you don't mind?"

"Plenty of time, and no, I don't mind," he said. "I just wish *we* had more time."

Freddie knew what that meant. Clay wanted more. More time, more lunches, more dinners, more walks on the beach. More of her.

And she wanted more, too. More than she deserved, more than she could bear. But she was so afraid giving in to him would only bring more heartache. But then, how could a man who had such a sweet, gentle nature ever hurt her, she wondered. How?

By leaving her here all alone, she reasoned.

And yet, she closed up shop, sent her workers home early and left to be with Clay.

Just for today.

The fall afternoon was crisp with the promise of cooler weather. The wind moved across the sea in a chase of light and splashes, while the sun slipped away like a slowly bouncing beach ball off behind the bay.

Everything was washed in a golden-hued light, as if someone had turned on a bedside lamp just in time for dusk to fall.

"That was a pretty good hamburger," Freddie said, grinning over at Clay. They were sitting on a wide deck on the beach near the boardwalk. She watched as Ryan frolicked down on a playground just off the deck, Samson barking as they played toss with a stick.

"Mike and Mike make the best food around, in my opinion," Clay said, jabbing another French fry into his mouth. "Now Stone, he goes for the fancy food—you know, lobster and caviar. Rock, he loves the Sunken Pier's seafood. But me, I'll take a Two-Mike burger over all of that any day."

Freddie shook her head. "So these two friends, both named Mike, decided to open a burger joint together?"

"That's right. Started as friendly cookouts in their yards. Then word started spreading about how good their burgers were. They wouldn't share their secret, so one of their friends suggested they open up a restaurant. That was twenty years ago. They've been right here, on this spot of beach, since then. They only take time off to play golf and go hunting occasionally." He waved a hand in the air as a waitress whizzed by. "As you can see, the tourists love this place."

Freddie had to agree. The deck had stayed packed with a steady stream of customers all afternoon. And all the tables inside the tiny wooden structure were full, too. "I'm going to gain a lot of weight, living here. First Miss McPherson's Brunswick stew and now, this monster of a hamburger. Ryan will want to eat here every day."

"I don't think a few pounds will hurt you," he said, an appreciative look on his face.

Freddie felt a little chill moving down her arms, but she couldn't say if it was from the wind pouring over them or Clay's eyes on her. She looked away, out over the water. "I feel safe here."

"I'm glad. How's the alarm system?"

"Good. If I can just remember to turn the thing off and on without causing a false alarm."

"And…what about those self-defense lessons? We never did set that up."

She thought about Todd's threats, thought about how her son missed his father's family. Then she thought about having Clay give her a refresher course on how to protect herself. "Maybe that wasn't such a good idea."

"I won't push you, Freddie."

She looked back at him, surprise causing her heart to skip. "What do you mean?"

"I mean, today I came on too strong. It's just that, well, it's just that it's hard…seeing you. I don't know. I haven't felt this way…well, I've never felt this way."

She wanted to tell him she felt the same. But she had to remind herself that she had to get her life in order before she could even begin to think about a love life again. But then, maybe she'd never really had a love life the first time around. She'd gone through the motions, tried to make her husband love her, but she'd never felt Gary's love. Only his disregard and distrust, his demands and his paranoia. What did love feel like?

Rock would tell her that real love came from God. Since God had never been in her relationship with Gary, Freddie found it hard to comprehend how God could be in the center of the love between a man and a woman. Yet she knew Rock was right. God was there in his relationship with Ana. And now Stone and Tara had put God first in their lives and they were happy, so happy.

What about me? she wondered now as she sat looking at Clay. *What about us? Could we be truly happy?*

"What?" Clay asked, his hand reaching across the cedar table to touch hers.

She gave him a bittersweet smile. "I was thinking that I've turned my life around, here on this island. I'm trying to be a better mother to my son. I'm trying to have a better life than the one I left behind."

"And you're also thinking that I can't be a part of that life, no matter how we might feel about each other?"

"I don't know," she said, hoping her honesty would make him see that she truly was confused. "I would like to think so, but..."

"But you're scared."

"Yes. I can't make another mistake. Ryan deserves better."

"Would it be a mistake to just enjoy each other?"

"It would be, if you plan on going back to Atlanta in a few weeks."

"Oh, I see. You think I'm just in town for a summer fling."

"Maybe?" She smiled again. "It would be hard to maintain a relationship, long-distance."

He nodded, frowned, kept his hand over hers. "Or, it might give us both some time to decide if this is worth exploring."

Freddie pulled her hand away. "You have that twinkle in your eyes."

"What twinkle?"

"The one you get when you're up to something. I know you well enough to know that, at least."

"I was just thinking that since we do have a few weeks, we could…see what develops."

"You mean, beyond friendship?"

"Maybe."

"And if nothing develops?"

"Then I'll be on my way back to Atlanta, knowing I have a friend to share time with whenever I come home to Sunset Island."

"How convenient for you."

"And you," he said, holding up his tea glass to salute her. "I mean, no strings, no pressure. Just someone to have fun with, share a few laughs, dance a few dances." Then he put his glass down and leaned close. "Someone to kiss now and then."

He looked as if he was going to do just that.

"I don't think kissing should be part of the bargain."

"But we'd need to explore all the…perks of this relationship, right?"

"Right. And one *perk* would be that *no pressure* part you just mentioned."

His hand was back on hers, his fingers tracing little swirls over her palm. His eyes were a charming, disarming sea blue, and his smile was…irresistible. "Kissing shouldn't be any pressure. It should be natural and fun, interesting and…enjoyable."

"It could complicate a perfectly good friendship."

"Or it could prove to us that we need to be together."

"A kiss?"

"Yeah, just one, now, for starters. Just to see—"

She leaned forward, about to give in by teasing him with a quick peck, but a sharp bark from Samson caused her to glance down at the shore. "Where's Ryan?"

She jumped up, pushing the bench she'd been sitting on across the floor, Clay right on her heels as they rushed down the planked steps and onto the crowded beach. "Ryan?"

Samson barked and alerted them, heading to the left, just out of their view.

"Where is he, boy?" Clay said, his voice sharp.

Samson barked and wagged his tail, looking back at them. "Show me," Clay said, following the dog.

Freddie called out again, her heart racing with a sickening thud as she thought of all the horrible things that could happen to a little boy. "Ryan? Ryan?"

She felt Clay's hand on her as she rushed up the beach. "It's okay. It's okay." He pointed to where Ryan was standing with a man by the white ice-cream booth set back from the beach.

"He's with Lee Fletcher."

"Lee?" Freddie heard her own question as if it were coming from inside a deep drum. Her pulse throbbed inside her head like a warning. She'd looked away for a split second and almost lost her son.

"Hey, it's okay," Clay said, still holding her arm. "Lee wouldn't hurt a fly. But he shouldn't have taken Ryan off like that."

"Ryan," she called as she ran toward her son.

Lee turned to grin at her. "Hi, there, boss. I saw the little fellow down on the beach and decided to buy him an ice-cream cone." Seeing the panic that Freddie was sure showed on her face, Lee gave her an apologetic look. "Ah, now, I'm sorry. I didn't mean to scare you. Just wanted to visit with my little buddy here."

"It's okay," Clay said, glancing over at Freddie. "Samson should have alerted us sooner."

"Oh, that big fellow," Lee said, laughing. "I've been around animals all my life, Clay. I knew a treat would calm him down. I threw him a stick to go fetch, then I gave him a doggie treat."

Freddie could see the anger clouding Clay's face like thunder moving over the ocean. "Lee, he's a trained K-9. You shouldn't distract him with treats. Samson knows the rules. I commanded him to stay. That's why he alerted me, thank goodness."

"He did bark at me," Lee said, unperturbed by the reprimand. "But I have a way with animals. I'm sure he thought I was playing stick toss with him. Doc can tell you. I have a way of calming animals down."

A chill raced over Freddie's body, making her shiver with fear and dread. Minutes ago, she'd felt safe. Now she felt raw and exposed. "Lee, Ryan isn't supposed to walk away with adults. Not without getting my permission."

Lee looked confused and embarrassed. "It's me, Doc. Me. I'd never harm this boy. You gotta know that."

Freddie saw the sincerity in the man's eyes, but she still didn't trust him. "I do believe that, Lee, and I'm sorry I panicked, but—"

"I'm okay, Mommy," Ryan said, his ice cream dripping down his chin and on his fingers. "Honest. Samson was watching out for me, and…I thought it would be okay to go with Lee. You said never to talk to strangers. But what about friends? Aren't friends allowed?"

Freddie fell in the sand, then hugged her son close, tears of relief misting her eyes. "Friends are allowed, baby, as long as you ask Mommy first. Next time, just come to me and let me decide whether you can have an ice cream or not, okay?"

"Okay," Ryan squeaked. "Mommy, you're gonna make me drop my ice cream."

Freddie pulled away, sniffed, then laughed. "I'll buy you another one."

Lee looked at her, his eyes full of concern. "I guess I'd better head on out. Sorry I scared you."

"Lee," she said, getting up, "I'm sorry I overreacted. It's just that…we're still new here and I don't quite know everyone."

"I understand," Lee said. He nodded to Clay, then ruffled Ryan's dark head. "See you, buddy."

"Okay. Thanks, Lee." Ryan munched his ice cream.

Samson gave a low bark as Lee walked by, obviously hoping for more play and treats.

"He didn't calm Samson down too much," Clay said through a long sigh. "Even though he threw Samson off a bit, Samson knew to come to us."

Freddie looked down at her son, then back to Clay. "Why would Lee be carrying around dog treats?"

"He works for you," Clay replied. "You tell me."

"Maybe he had one or two in his pocket," Freddie reasoned, an uneasiness settling around her as darkness fell.

"But you don't believe that?"

"I'm just being paranoid."

"Well, maybe you can answer a question for me then," Clay said as they headed toward his truck. "Why *are* you being so paranoid, Freddie? What's really going on? I saw the way you panicked when you thought Ryan was lost. Why don't you tell me the truth, so I can help you? Why don't you tell me who's got you so scared?"

Chapter Nine

She hadn't told him anything.

Clay ran alongside Freddie on the beach, Samson following them as they went through a morning jog. They'd been doing this for the last week, running, practicing kickboxing out at Stone's gym at Hidden Hill, swimming laps in the big pool, going over the standard self-defense techniques that Freddie already knew, doing everything to get her in top shape and well prepared to take care of herself.

And still, she'd never told Clay why she seemed so intent on doing this.

As they came to the curve in the island where the ocean met the bay, Clay stopped to bend down and catch his breath, his eyes on Freddie as she did the same. This was the turning-around point. They always stopped right here, just to the left of the lighthouse.

Clay felt as if this might be a turning point in their relationship, too. So he sent Samson to chase after a washed-up piece of driftwood, then asked the question burning inside him. "Why are you doing this, Freddie?"

She looked up, that stark fear clear in her dark eyes. Tossing her braid over her shoulder, she shrugged and wiped at her forehead with her wristband. "I told you—"

"Yeah, you told me you just want to feel secure, safe. I can understand that. But you never did answer my question the other day, after Ryan gave us that scare."

She sighed, jogged in place for a couple of seconds. "Clay, we're friends, right?"

"Yes." And more. He needed more. But he didn't say that. "But you don't trust me enough to tell me what's really eating at you."

"It's personal," she said, her eyes turning a soft, deep brown.

Clay felt a slight shift in her defenses, as if she really wanted to tell him, but was afraid. "You know you can trust me, don't you?"

"I'm beginning to see that, yes."

"Okay." He did a couple of stretches, the still-healing muscles in his left shoulder shouting in protest. Clay ignored that particular reminder, his eyes on Freddie, his mind on her problems. "Let me take a guess at this. You're afraid your in-laws are going to come after Ryan, right?"

He saw the answer in her eyes. Freddie sank down

on a jutting terrace of sea-washed land, then looked out over the foaming water. Samson came running to her, ready for an instant pat on the head. "I almost forgot," she said in a low, gravelly voice as her hand moved over Samson's ears, "that cops have really good instincts."

"Yeah, well, my instincts tell me that I'm right."

"You are right," she finally said. "It's my brother-in-law, Todd. He…he wants to see Ryan and he's threatened to come here and demand that I allow him to do just that. But then, you already knew part of this."

Clay's heart hit at his ribs with an angry beat. "Yeah, but you didn't tell me all of it. He's threatened you?"

"Not in so many words. He just wants to see Ryan. And I can understand that. But I've asked for some time. *I* need more time."

Clay heard the fear in that gentle plea. "Why can't the man understand that?"

She shrugged, looked down at her running shoes. "Todd is a very angry man. He's a cop, too, remember? And so is his father. It runs in the family, this anger toward the world."

"Wow." Clay sank down beside her. "That puts a whole new light on things." Then he glanced over at her. "And are Todd and his father like Gary? Are they corrupt?"

"To the core," she said, the relief of saying it draining her face to a pale porcelain. "That's why they left Georgia and moved out west. They've kind of burned all their bridges here. And that's why I'm so worried. They…they might take the law into their own hands, if you get my drift."

Clay nodded, his expression grim. "I get it, all right." But he didn't intend to let that happen. "Look," he said, hoping to reassure her, "you know you can count on me, right? You must know that, since you turned to me to help you with security and self-defense."

She nodded, but her eyes didn't hold any hope. "I wondered at the wisdom of even getting you involved, but since you're a policeman, I felt you were the best choice to help me. And I guess that's just a throwback to the days I depended on Gary for so much. But I have to do things on my own now, so that's all I need right now. Just some advice. I can't depend on you any further than that, Clay. That's why…that's the reason I've been pushing you away."

Realization dawned over Clay like the morning sun coming in over the ocean. "Because you want to prove something, or because you think I'll just up and leave in a few weeks?"

"It's not so much that, although you do have to go back to Atlanta eventually. It's just that, well, I have to do this on my own. I *do* need to prove it—to myself. You have to understand—I depended on Gary for everything, on so many levels. And he expected me to be dependent on him. When I started being more assertive and more confident in my own abilities, things got very tense between us. I lost the man I'd always loved long before he died, but I didn't realize until after his death that what we had wasn't really love. It was some sort of codependency. I won't go through that again, with anyone."

Clay moved a little closer. "So you think that by letting me into your life completely, that by admitting how we really feel about each other, you'll wind up depending on another man too much? And that man might let you down?"

"Something like that." She wouldn't look at him, but she didn't move away. "Rock says we have to depend on the Lord above all else, so that's what I'm trying to do. I'm trying to put God first, and Ryan, too. I have to protect Ryan. I want him to remember the good things about his father and his family back in Dallas. So that's why I need time—time away from Todd, and away from Ryan's other grandparents, and time away from—"

"Away from a heavy relationship?"

She looked over at him then, her smile tender and full of longing. "Yes. You are a good, decent man, and I could easily fall for you. But…I came here with a certain purpose. I have to focus on that purpose."

Clay understood what she was saying, but her lips looked so inviting, he pushed her statement out of his mind. "What if I have a purpose?"

"And what would that be, besides getting Samson and yourself healed?"

He leaned close, his hand touching on the thick braid of hair roping around her neck. She smelled like the ocean, salty and sweet at the same time. "This," he said. Before she could move, he touched his lips to hers in a soft, gentle kiss that washed him with a new longing, a new purpose, a new intention.

She didn't pull away. Freddie sank against him, her hands curving around his neck. Her touch was warm and inviting, firm but tentative. Clay deepened the kiss, pulled her closer, took his time enjoying the way she sighed in his arms.

And then, like a wave moving back out to sea, the mood was gone.

Freddie jumped up, shock evident on her face as she backed away. "That was not supposed to happen."

Clay saw the way she put distance between them, watched as her expression changed from content and fulfilled to confused and angry, and he regretted that she couldn't allow her feelings to show.

Hurt and angry, he got up, pushed a hand over his hair. "Then it won't happen again." He whistled to Samson, then turned to throw her a glance over his shoulder. "We'd better get back. You've got to get to work and I've got things to take care of."

With that, he took off toward town. They'd reached a turning point, all right.

And maybe, the point of no return.

She'd hurt him.

Freddie stared down at the papers on her desk, not seeing the charts and folders Kate had placed in front of her ten minutes ago. She kept thinking about Clay and that kiss. He'd kissed her right there on the beach.

And her heart had crashed against all the powerful feelings that kiss had stirred inside her soul. Her heart had fought a battle of wills with her head, but her sensibilities had won out over her heart's longing.

"It can't happen again."

She didn't even realize she'd spoken out loud until she looked up to see Lee Fletcher standing in the doorway of her office, a questioning look on his craggy face. "You say something, Doc?"

"Oh, just mumbling to myself," Freddie said by way of an explanation. "Is it time to go home?"

"Past," Lee said as he slumped into a chair. "Hey, Doc, about the other day—you know, when I bought Ryan that ice cream—"

"It's okay, Lee, really." Freddie felt bad that Lee now seemed uncomfortable around her. "I just overreacted."

"No, I was wrong to take the boy off without telling you," Lee said, holding up a bronzed hand. "Scout's honor, it won't happen again. But if you ever need me, for anything, you just let me know."

"I will," Freddie said, touched by the sincerity in the man's eyes. "And I promise I won't panic like that again, as long as you promise to let me know next time my son has a hankering for an ice-cream cone."

"Promise," Lee said, clearly relieved that they'd cleared that up. "I sure like that little fellow. He's smart as a whip and well, I know what it's like to not have a daddy around."

"I'm sorry," Freddie said. "Did your father die when you were young?"

"Never knew my father," Lee replied, a blank look in his stark blue eyes. "That's why I used to tell those crazy Dempsey boys that they were lucky to have known their father for a little while at least. Mine never acknowledged me."

Freddie felt a chill rushing down her spine. Lee looked so lost and forlorn, she wondered just what the man had suffered. "I am sorry, Lee. Ryan did know his father for a little while, too. I have to remember the good times and remind my son of that, at least."

"You'd be wise to do that," Lee said. Then the laughter came back into his eyes. "Well, I'm off for a sail into the sunset. Want to come?"

"No, thanks," Freddie said, shuffling the papers in front of her. "I'm going to finish up these files, then call it a day. I think Ryan and I are going to work on his homework, then get to bed early. He's loves his new school here, so it's kind of hard to get him to wind down every night."

"Well, more power to the little fellow. Me, I never liked school that much." Lee laughed, then waved as he headed out the door.

Freddie stared after him, again wondering what had molded and shaped her capable helper into the lonely man he was today. She didn't want Ryan to wind up lonely and bitter because of her decisions. Maybe she should let him see his uncle and his grandparents. Maybe that would be the best thing for everyone.

But just the thought of going back to Texas, even for a short visit, left her feeling sick at her stomach. Freddie thought of Clay again. Even if they couldn't let things go any further between them, at least she could remember the sweetness of his kiss to help her through the rough times.

No, not just the kiss, she told herself, remembering how he made her laugh, how he always had an easy solution to the worst of problems. They'd spent a lot of time together over the last couple of weeks, so she had a pretty good idea of who Clay Dempsey really was. And he was nothing like Gary Hayes. Clay was easygoing and cautious, but smart and sure of himself. He was well-trained to help her get in shape, but not so macho and overbearing that she dreaded learning from him. Clay was being exactly what she'd asked him to be, a reliable, steady friend. He was good with animals and children, too, and that counted in Freddie's book. He was also a good kisser, she reminded herself. And that *definitely* counted in her book. Even now, the memory of his touch brought little tingles down her spine, tingles that felt like warm water hitting her nerve endings.

She wished she could rely on these exciting, unexplainable feelings. But she wouldn't rely on anything beyond her memories. But oh, how she wished she could just let go and enjoy all these new sensations swirling through her like a waterfall.

She'd hurt Clay, though. And she had a feeling he wouldn't forget that hurt so easily. What if she'd lost the best friend she'd ever had?

"I can't let that happen," she said as she finished up and started for the door. "I have to make him understand."

She intended to have a talk with Clay Dempsey, just to make the man see reason, at least.

"She has her reasons, I guess," Clay told Rock the next night. "Freddie just doesn't want anything more than friendship right now." He didn't tell his brother how much she'd hurt him by rejecting his kiss. Well, she didn't exactly reject the kiss, just him. And for that reason, he'd been avoiding her ever since. "I have to respect that. I can be her friend, I think." *Once I get over this disappointment.*

Rock looked doubtful, but thankfully kept his voice low so his mother and Ana wouldn't jump on this intriguing news. "Are you sure about that, Clay? You looked pretty whipped when you got here tonight."

They were having dinner with Eloise and her friend, widower Don Ashworth, something that happened a lot these days. Clay was still amazed that his mother had become so maternal and domestic, and actually had a "male" friend. He wasn't used to family dinners and long talks over coffee and pie.

"I'm tired," Clay said in answer to Rock's concern. "I've tried to stay busy making sure Samson goes through his paces with his therapy. I want him to get a good report when we go back for his next checkup. If he doesn't—"

"Will you have to find a new partner?"

Clay nodded. "Either that, or find a new job."

Rock sat up in his chair, then glanced back toward the kitchen where Eloise and Ana were laughing and talking to Cy and Neda as they cleared the dinner dishes. "What's that mean? You're not thinking of leaving the force?"

Clay took a sip of his coffee, then finished off his chocolate pie. "Not exactly. Just thinking of maybe leaving the city. Maybe finding something a little more relaxed and laid-back."

Rock's eyebrows shot up. "Like…Sunset Island, for example?"

Clay grinned then. "Okay, maybe. I have been spending some time down at the island patrol station. Half the four-man force here is ready to retire, and the other half doesn't seem to care either way. It's tempting."

Rock nodded. "Tell me about it. We don't have much crime, but earlier this summer when one of Tara's daughters was missing, Chief Anderson didn't seem too worried. Mother had to practically force him to go out and look for her and Cal. We'd all like to see *that* man retire, trust me."

"But do you think I could do a good job here?"

Rock's eyes lit up. "I think you'd do a wonderful job, brother. But what about Samson?"

"We're partners for life. He'd be right here with me," Clay said, holding up a hand toward his brother's obvious approval, "if I decided to do that, of course."

"Do what?" Eloise said as she entered the big, breezy parlor after telling Don Ashworth good-night. She always kept the windows open as much as possible and tonight, the crisp autumn wind was whipping around the lace curtains. It lifted her short hair toward her face as she smiled down at her sons. "What's up?"

"Oh, just considering what to do with the rest of my vacation. Only about a week or so left," Clay said, hoping she'd let the subject drop.

She didn't.

"I think you'll probably spend the rest of your time with Freddie Hayes, right?"

Clay ignored the beam of hope in his mother's silver eyes. But then Ana took up the slack.

"Yes, and why didn't you invite Freddie and Ryan to dinner tonight?" Ana asked, one hand on her hip as she glared at both Clay and her husband.

"Don't look at me," Rock said. "I mentioned this get-together to Freddie in church Sunday. She said she had plans."

"Clay?"

Clay put down his empty coffee cup, then cut to the

chase. "Freddie doesn't like being set up. We'd both appreciate it if all of you well-meaning people would just back off."

"We haven't done anything," Eloise said, sitting down with an elaborate fluffing of her gathered linen skirts. "Have we, Ana?"

"No, nothing more than being neighborly and polite," Ana said, her eyes brimming with mirth. "And we can't help it if Greta Epperson is always calling us, wanting to know why you're spending so much time with the new vet, now can we, Clay?"

"And just what do you tell the fair Greta?" Clay asked, an uneasy feeling settling right along with his pie.

"We tell her exactly what you always say, that Freddie and you are just good friends."

"Good friends who like to take long walks on the beach and spend time out at Hidden Hill by the pool," Eloise added, her smile serene and smug.

"We're giving Samson therapy," Clay said. Then he shrugged and got up. "I give up. Look, Freddie has made it pretty clear she's not interested in me in a romantic way. Why don't you tell that to Greta next time she wants an exclusive?" Waving a hand in the air, he added, "I'm taking Samson for his walk."

"Clay?" Eloise rushed after him as he headed up the long hallway. "I'm sorry. We didn't mean to tease."

He turned to stare down at his mother, the stark beauty of her face making him remember other nights when he'd needed her to rush after him. "I don't want Freddie to think…to think I'm stifling her, Mother. She needs some time and some space right now. I'm trying to respect that."

"And what about you?" Eloise asked, concern shifting the light from her eyes. "Do you need more time and space, too?"

"Yes, I guess I do," Clay admitted. "I need to make some decisions about…things. So, please, just let this go for now."

"All right," Eloise said, her hand on his arm. "No more questions, no more teasing. I just wish—"

"I know what you wish, Mother," Clay said. "But I've been out there on my own for a long time now. I think I can figure this one out by myself."

He saw the flare of hurt and guilt in his mother's eyes and regretted the implications of that statement. But it was the truth. "I'm sorry," he said on a raspy voice.

"No, no," Eloise held up a hand, her bracelets moving down her arm in a tinkling path. "You always were very independent and single-minded. But you also always put others first. And that's what you're doing now. I appreciate that in you, Son."

Clay hugged his mother close, hoping to bridge the distance between them. "And I appreciate that you're trying to make up for…so many things, Mother. But let me find my own way with Freddie, okay?"

"Okay." Eloise stepped back, her smile bittersweet. "I'll say prayers for proper guidance."

Prayers.

Clay could use a few of those. He'd come home hoping to find answers for the questions that had been nagging him since the night both he and Samson had gotten hurt. But he still didn't have any answers. In fact, he was now more confused than ever.

He could use his mother's prayers.

And he'd sure say a few of his own. Maybe that was what was holding him back. He'd forgotten to turn things over to God. Clay wanted to control his life, wanted to make Freddie see that he was falling for her, but he knew that sometimes prayers weren't answered in the way people wanted them to be answered.

And yet, he said a prayer as Samson and he walked up the beach on their evening stroll. He prayed for Freddie.

Let her see that I'm not like him, Lord.

Protect her.

Help her.

Give her a reason to find joy again.

And give me a reason to go back to Atlanta.

Or…a reason to stay on Sunset Island.

Chapter Ten

"Honey, you don't have to have a reason to visit me. And you sure don't have to call ahead. You know I'm going to always be here."

Freddie smiled over at her father, understanding that his words were sincere, and realizing, too, that he wouldn't be able to always be here. Her mother was gone. Gary was gone. Her father was the only close relative she had left. And apparently, since Clay hadn't called her since their last jogging session three days ago, she'd managed to drive her new best friend away, too. Which only proved she just couldn't live on promises anymore, even from her sweet father. Yet, she couldn't say that to him, either.

"We just wanted to spend the day with you, Daddy," she said as he handed her a glass of his special hand-squeezed lemonade.

"Well, I'm glad. But you sounded a bit frantic when you called."

Wade Noble was still a very distinguished-looking man, even if he was in his seventies. He lived a simple life, here in the brick ranch house he's shared with her mother for over thirty-five years. Freddie appreciated the way he'd saved little things of her mother's, to pass on to her and Ryan one day. He hadn't changed the house that much, but he'd learned to live and move on without his wife. Never one to be domestic before, he now cooked and cleaned and stayed busy volunteering at his church, and he worked part-time at various odd jobs around the small community that had been his home all of his life. As much as he missed her mother, Wade Noble had a kind of peace about him that spoke of a deep, abiding faith that would take him into eternity.

Freddie could take a lesson from that.

"Oh, I'm okay," she said now in answer to his concerned statement. "Just busy at work. I didn't mean to worry you. It's just…good to see you, Dad," she said as she hugged him close. They stood on the back patio, watching Ryan as he played in a brand-new kiddy pool his grandfather had bought especially for him.

"So how are things on Sunset Island?" her father asked, his expression telling her he wanted to get to the bottom of this sudden visit.

"Work is good. I have a great office manager, a cute

college student named Kate. She's planning on becoming a veterinarian herself one day. And I have a crusty helper who continues to amaze me. Lee has such a way with animals." She thought back over her talk with Lee Fletcher earlier in the week, worry causing her to frown.

"But?"

"But what?" she asked, seeing the questions in her father's hazel eyes.

"But…something is bothering you. I could always tell when you needed to have a heart-to-heart talk."

Freddie laughed. "How so?"

"You'd come into the den and just sit there. Much in the way you're just standing here right now. I mean, you had to drive a couple of hours, but here you are. Is this Lee fellow giving you trouble?"

Freddie laughed, then sank down onto a cushioned deck chair. "Okay, you got me. I do need to talk, but it's not about Lee. He's a good worker, a bit odd, but he's the least of my problems right now."

Wade sat down next to her, his eyes on his grandson. Ryan splashed water at them with a giant water gun, just missing Freddie's sandaled foot. "Hey, watch it, buddy."

Ryan grinned, then flopped into the shallow water.

Freddie turned her attention back to her patient father. "I've met someone."

"Oh, I see." His look was full of gentle encouragement and maybe a bit of resolve. "Is this good or bad, this 'meeting someone'?"

"Mostly good," she said, meaning it. "He's very nice. Clay truly fits the description of a good guy. He's from a family that's been on the island for generations. He's been helping me with some things—security for my cottage, working out to stay in shape. And I've been helping him with his dog, Samson. Therapy."

"Therapy." Wade let that word settle in the still afternoon air. "When you say he's a good man, does that mean—"

"He's a Christian, Daddy. His whole family—well, they're all loving Christian people. In every sense of the word."

"That's good to hear," Wade said, relaxing back against his chair. He lowered his gaze, but not before Freddie saw the relief in his eyes.

"Not like Gary, you want to say."

"I didn't mention any names."

"But I know how you felt about him."

"I kept my opinions to myself."

"And I appreciate that about you," Freddie told her father. "You tried so hard to be a friend to Gary, through it all. You tried to be a father to him."

"But he resented that," Wade reminded her. "I think that's why he took you to Dallas after Ryan was born. Just to get away from me."

"He wanted to be near his family," Freddie said, amazed that she still felt the need to defend Gary. "And the job offer there was a good one. We both found jobs there."

"But all of that aside, he didn't want any part of your mother and me," Wade said, shrugging, his voice low. "I hope Ryan will be different."

"He will," Freddie said, leaning forward. "I intend to raise Ryan in the church. He's already involved with the church community on Sunset Island. And he loves it. He's really basking in all the positive attention."

"That's a relief," Wade said, grinning toward his grandson. "He sure seems happy and healthy."

"He is. We are," Freddie said, wanting to reassure her father. She couldn't bring herself to tell him about Todd's threatening phone calls.

Wade glanced back over at her. "You seem content, too, honey. It's good to see you smiling again. Now, tell me, does this Clay person have anything to do with that?"

Freddie nodded, sighed. "Yes and no." If she could just get up the nerve to apologize to Clay for pushing him away, she'd be a whole lot more content right now. But first, she needed some fatherly advice. "I don't think dating Clay is such a good idea, so I kind of told him to back off. Only now, I think that was a big mistake."

Wade looked confused. "Okay, you're gonna have to explain that, young lady."

"Clay's a cop, Dad," Freddie said.

"I see." Wade sank back, a deflated look on his aged face. "Well, that certainly complicates things, now, doesn't it?"

"It's complicated," Clay told Rock that night. "I care about Freddie, a lot. I'd like to get to know her even more, but she doesn't want to get involved with a cop, and I have to go back to Atlanta soon. That doesn't leave much room for a romantic relationship."

They were on the beach in front of Hidden Hill. Rock had been watching while Clay went through a round of tug-of-war with Samson. Now as dusk began to fall over the water, the dog was content to stroll along the shore while his master took a break.

"Relationships often are complicated," Rock commented as he tossed Clay a bottle of water from a small cooler. "You two sure look good together. It's too bad you can't work all of this out." He stood silent for a minute, then glanced up at the big mansion on the hill. "Why are you staying here, Clay? Mother would have liked you to stay with her."

"I have stayed with her," Clay said, his tone steady and firm, even though his brother had changed the subject with a heartbeat. Knowing Rock, however, Clay suspected there was a reason his brother had done that. "I spent one night last week with her. We had a good long talk, well into the wee hours."

"You know what I mean," Rock replied. "One night doesn't make up for—"

Clay shrugged, holding up a hand to stop his brother. "It doesn't make up for all the nights she worked late in her studio, does it?"

"You do resent her."

"Yeah, I guess I do," Clay admitted. "I guess it never surfaced until…until I almost died."

Rock motioned to the jutting land just beyond the shore, where the sand met the grass and trees. "Let's sit a spell."

Clay whistled to Samson. The big dog came running, anxious for another game. They found a shady spot underneath a towering live oak drenched with Spanish moss. Clay told Samson to sit. Reluctantly, the dog plopped down at Clay's feet, his big brown eyes asking for a scratch behind the ears. Clay obliged him, his gaze on Samson as he debated how much to tell his brother. But he needed to talk. He needed to get his head clear. Maybe confession was good for the soul. "I didn't see it coming."

Rock looked over at him, no censure or condemnation in his eyes. Clay saw then why his brother was such a good preacher. Rock listened to people. Really listened. He was willing to listen to his little brother now.

"The suspect had dropped the gun. I'd saved Samson from getting shot—or rather he'd saved me—but when we all fell down that shaft together, well, the suspect managed to get his hands on a piece of rebar. He sent it through my left shoulder. And I managed to shoot him before he could finish the job."

He heard Rock's hiss of breath. "You told us it was a flesh wound, nothing more."

"It was a wound, that's for sure," Clay said. "I didn't want y'all to worry."

"Same as when we were growing up," Rock said, nodding. "You never wanted to worry anyone with your troubles. You never complained."

Clay turned to his brother then, his fist going to his chest. "It was all here, inside me, Rock. It was all right here."

Rock nodded again, compassion clear in his blue eyes. "And now, it feels like a weight pushing against your chest, crushing your soul?"

Clay managed one word between the thick lump in his throat. "Yes." He swallowed, looked out to sea. "What's wrong with me, brother?"

Rock clapped a hand on his back. "You almost died, Clay. That tends to make a man stop and think."

"I had plenty of time to think, all right. I thought about the kid I'd killed in the line of duty. He was only sixteen. He was just a gofer for the top dogs. They'd sent him to move the stash. A way to prove his manhood or something. Now he'll never be a man. He's dead."

"You killed him in self-defense," Rock reminded him.

But the pain of all of it still burned just as badly as that piece of jagged steel going through his skin. "How do I get past that, though? How do I get past everything I thought about while I was lying in that hospital room?"

"You came home," Rock said, his tone gentle. "That's a start."

"Is it a start?" Clay asked, his hand stopping on Samson's head. "Or is it an end?"

"It could be a new beginning," Rock replied. "A fresh start, a new lease on life."

"I didn't die," Clay said, shrugging. "I didn't die that night."

"And you wonder why you lived and that kid had to die?"

"Yeah." Clay bobbed his head. "I keep thinking I don't deserve anything. I don't deserve being closer to our mother, or being home here on this island. I don't deserve…I don't deserve a woman like Freddie."

Rock sat still, staring out toward the foaming water. "There is a Proverb that states the beginning of strife is like the releasing of water. You had a crisis, Clay. And now you need to let go and start living again. You survived the worst a man can survive. You're still grieving, still in shock. Let it go, brother. Release this strife that's brought you to a standstill."

"How do I do that?"

Rock pointed up toward the rising night, toward the heavens. "You know the answer to that."

Clay nodded, lowered his head. "And Freddie?"

"Freddie will see you for the man you are," Rock said, his steady gaze like a beacon to his brother. "You're a good man, Clay. As sure and steady as this ocean. I truly believe you will find your way."

Clay breathed deeply, inhaling the salty, misty air of sunset and sea foam. "It is good to be home. I think I'm beginning to heal, really heal, at last."

"You need to tell Mother all of this," Rock said as they headed up the stone-covered path back to the mansion. "And…you need to tell Freddie. She won't trust you until you open up your heart to her, Clay. She needs to know you are an honest, honorable man."

"Am I that?"

"You, little brother, are all that and more. And you do deserve to be happy. God wants that for you, Clay."

"Trial by fire?"

"Maybe. Or maybe because you *have* always been so easygoing and dependable, God knew you'd get through this test and become a better man."

"God sure is tough on us."

"He only gives us what He knows we can stand."

"I've had enough for now, brother."

"Then tell Him that. Ask Him to take over."

"By letting go."

Rock nodded again, then grinned. "Let it go. Let the water purge you clean."

Clay listened to his brother, listened to the wind and

the waves. "I just feel as if…there's something more, something just around the bend. Another test for me."

Rock turned on the path. "Face it. Embrace it. And get through it. Move that mountain. 'Man cannot remake himself without suffering. For he is both the marble and the sculptor'—Alexis Carrel."

Clay understood his brother's philosophy. "I've been shaped and molded by…so many things. Now it's time for me to reshape myself, to test my strength, right?"

"You have the strength, Clay. You've had it all along. Now, with God's help, you can use it to overcome this crisis in your life. You are the potter's clay."

Clay closed his eyes and thought of Freddie. It was time to be honest with her. Time to take things one step further. Time to move on and get on with his life. His new life. His new beginning.

But before he could do that, he had to make peace with his mother. And with himself.

Chapter Eleven

"I come in peace," Clay said to his mother the next morning. He found her in her studio bent over what looked like a lump of modeling clay.

Eloise looked up, surprise and pleasure both apparent in her silver eyes. "My youngest son! What brings you here?" She waved her arms. "You rarely come into my studio."

"You are so correct," Clay said, giving Samson a command to stay outside the big open double doors. Clay hesitated a couple of seconds before pushing off the doorjamb to move farther into the chaotic, cluttered room. He watched his mother as she automatically went back to her work, her hands moving over the moist gray lump with precision. "Mother, I came for a reason. I need you to listen to me."

Eloise's hands stopped moving. She lifted them

away from the work in progress, then turned to find a wipe rag. "Okay. Your serious tone has certainly gotten my attention, Son."

"That's what I need," Clay said, wondering how he was going to go about this gentle confrontation. "I *need* your attention. In fact, I've reached a very obvious conclusion over the last few days. I've always needed your attention."

Eloise sank back against a wooden workbench, her eyes going misty as she stared up at him. "You know, I've reached that same conclusion, too. It's funny, when you were all children, I thought you could learn responsibility and character if I gave you a solid faith foundation, but also allowed you free will. Now that you're all men, I've found that you do need boundaries." She came over to Clay then, touched a putty-splattered hand to his face. "You need the boundaries of a mother's love…and attention."

Clay felt the warmth of her hand on his face, remembered how she'd tucked him in at night, remembered the gentle love he'd seen in her eyes when she thought no one was watching. "You were afraid to love us too much, weren't you, Mother?"

Eloise nodded, swallowed, looked out over the moss-draped live oaks. A huge palmetto plant swayed just off the small patio beyond the doors. "Yes. I've never admitted that to anyone, especially myself. But after your father died…I was afraid of a lot of things."

Clay took her hand in his, stared down at it. She had

the hands of a true artist, long fingered and lithe. "When did you stop being afraid?"

Eloise squeezed his hand tightly in hers. "When I realized that if I didn't show my boys how much I loved them, I'd lose them forever anyway, one way or another."

Clay nodded, her statement echoing with a precise parallel the fear he felt in his own heart. He let go of her hand. Spinning around, he held his back to her for a minute, then turned to face her again. "I…never wanted to resent you, but I can see now that I did. I do."

"I know," she said, leaning back against the security of her workbench again. "I can see it in your eyes, in your policeman's stance. But I think you came home to remedy all of that."

Clay let out a grunt of final resistance, then plunged ahead. "I came close to dying that night, Mother. But I didn't want to worry you with the details."

She looked shocked for just a minute, then went back to her serene stance. "You always were the protector, the one who didn't want to bother or worry anyone else."

She stepped forward then and put her arms around him. "Let me worry, Clay. Let me worry for you, please."

Clay hugged his mother close. "Do you want to hear the whole story?"

"Yes, oh, yes," Eloise said, returning his hug before

she looked up at him with concern. "I want details. I know it will scare me and make me afraid for you, but I also know that I need to be involved in your life, good and bad. I'll just have to trust the Lord with the rest."

Clay laughed then. "There's a lot of bad, but…I'm beginning to think there might be some good in my future. And *I'm* going to trust the Lord regarding that good."

"You mean Freddie?"

"Yes, Mother, I mean Freddie. You were right all along."

"Mothers always know these things."

Clay grinned then. "Let's go sit in your garden. And I'll tell you everything."

"And will you forgive me?" Eloise asked.

"It's not about forgiveness, Mother. It's about finally seeing the truth and facing it head-on."

"That's my Clay," Eloise said, nodding her approval. "I'm so glad you came home, and that you finally came to me to make peace."

"I've had a very peaceful week," Freddie told Clay a few days later. "Our little kitty—Ryan named him BoBo—has settled down at the cottage, making himself right at home, and most of my appointments for this week were just routine checkups. No emergencies." She grinned, tipped her tea glass toward him. "And then, a handsome man asks me out to dinner. A nice ending to a good week, I'd say."

She wouldn't say how relieved she'd been to hear from him, how her heart had fluttered and pulsed back to life when he'd called. How glad she was that he seemed to be over his anger and hurt and back to being the interesting, easygoing man she'd come to care about as a good friend. *And maybe more.*

"Great. Let's celebrate with dessert," Clay replied, a twinkle in his eyes.

"I don't know where you put all that food," she said, giving him an appreciative look.

They were back at their favorite hangout, Two Mikes. Clay had just downed a cheeseburger with fries and a milkshake. Freddie had eaten a grilled-chicken sandwich and fries with tea. Now Clay had his eye on a fat piece of Key lime pie sitting in the cooler behind the counter.

"I'll half it with you," he promised, his eyes lighting up like a little kid's.

Freddie couldn't resist him. And she loved Key lime pie. "Okay. I guess we have been working out enough to burn off the extra calories."

Clay waved to the waitress, then pointed to the pie. "Two forks," he told the grinning woman. "And two cups of coffee." Turning back to Freddie, he nodded. "Yep. I'd say you're in the best shape possible. At least, it looks that way to me." He returned the same look she'd given him earlier. "How's the security system?"

"It's great," she told him, conscious of the way his

approving gaze moved over her. "And I can actually pay the bill I got the other day. Your friend gave me a fair price, based on your good name, he told me. It's easy to set and...I feel very safe now."

His expression changed to serious. "And what about your brother-in-law? Any more phone calls?"

"No, not from him," she said, a breath of relief leaving her body. Waiting until their waitress finished putting down their pie and coffees, she looked over at Clay. "But Pearl called. That's Todd's mother."

"Ryan's grandmother."

"Yes. She was nicer about things. Wanted me to know that they love and miss Ryan. She promised she would talk to Todd, explain to him that I'm not trying to keep Ryan away from them."

"Think she meant it?"

Freddie took a bite of the citrus-flavored, creamy pie. "Yes, I do. Pearl stands behind her son and her husband, only because they're both so domineering, but I believe when push comes to shove, she'll make them see reason."

"I hope so, for your sake. And for Ryan. That kid doesn't need to be caught up in family squabbles."

"No, I don't want him exposed to that. He saw enough just watching his father and me fight."

"He's young. He'll forget all of that."

Freddie saw the dark drift passing like clouds over water through Clay's eyes. "Did you forget the bad parts?"

He finished off his half of the pie, then shrugged. "I somehow managed to effectively block them out. Until recently."

Freddie poured cream into her coffee, then took a sip. She'd been surprised to hear from Clay after the way they'd left things with that kiss several days ago. And she hadn't gotten up the nerve to tell him she was sorry. Maybe because she wasn't so sorry about the kiss, just sorry that they couldn't take things further.

"What do you mean?" she asked, wondering if she'd been part of the reason for this sudden bitterness.

Clay sat silent, his fingers drumming on the wooden table. They were out on the deck. He glanced out at the water just beyond the boardwalk. "Want to go for a stroll along the shore?"

She saw the determined glint in his eyes. He'd been determined in his request that they have a real date tonight. He'd even supplied her with a baby-sitter for Ryan—his mother.

And Eloise had been very gracious and accommodating, promising Ryan all sorts of adventures inside her rambling Victorian house, Samson included for extra enticement. Her matchmaking abilities were becoming more and more obvious.

As was Clay's aggressive need to spend time with Freddie. He must have been serious tonight, since he'd left his faithful companion behind just so they could be alone. And in spite of her resolve to keep things uncomplicated, Freddie had been thrilled to hear from him.

"I could go for a walk in the moonlight," she told him, thinking she should just thank him and go home. But she didn't want to go home to an empty house and more worries. For just tonight, while the harvest moon was full and the water was dark and glistening, she wanted to walk along the beach with this man. Only this man. Only for tonight. No apologies, no resistance. Just companionship and happiness, to make up for how she'd treated him the last time they'd been together.

Clay laid two crisp tens down on the table, waved good-night to the two Mikes and their waitress, then took Freddie by the hand. "Let's go."

She could feel the energy coursing through him. Could feel the pulse of his heartbeat against her skin as he tugged her down the planked steps leading to the shore.

"What a perfect night," he said, his words husky and intimate as he pulled her close to ward off the crisp evening chill. "It's like that moon is hanging there just for us."

"Did you plan that?"

He grinned over at her, the look in his eyes stating that he had lots of big plans. Freddie had to catch her breath. This was very dangerous, this being with Clay Dempsey on a daily basis. Before their fight, they had jogged and worked out each morning with the sun rising behind them, and on certain afternoons, they'd worked with Samson while Ryan swam nearby in the big pool at Hidden Hill, Freddie and Clay laughing and splashing and talking about nothing, but saying everything. They'd spent evenings together here and there, under small pretenses that spoke volumes about how they were feeling. How they were beginning to depend on each other. Until he'd kissed her. Then all of that had come to a sudden halt.

Freddie had missed him immediately, had wanted to call him. But common sense had told her not to depend on Clay, so as much as she wanted to explain things to him, she'd stalled and held back.

I can't depend on him, she reminded herself. *He's a cop. Plain and simple. And for a cop, the job always came first.*

Somehow, she had to make Clay understand why she kept pushing him away.

But when Clay turned to her and pulled her close, his eyes holding hers there in the shimmering light of a creamy yellow moon, she felt as if she'd come home to the security and safety she'd always craved and needed. It wasn't easy for Freddie to admit that. She'd always been independent and strong, in spite of Gary's need to change her and mold her. That need for independence had been the downfall in her marriage.

It might also prove to be the downfall in her growing feelings for Clay.

"What's wrong?" he said, as if he could sense her fear and her doubts. "Are you still stewing about that kiss?"

"Are you still angry with me about that kiss?"

"I was at first. But then, I got over it." He looked out at the waves lifting in a timeless dance. "So what's bugging you tonight?"

"Nothing and everything," she admitted, liking the way his instincts seemed to keep things in tune, in spite of not wanting him to know her true feelings. "That's the problem. Nothing is wrong, but everything could go wrong. This is too good, Clay."

He nuzzled her neck, his lips touching on her like a warm breeze skipping over her skin. "What's so wrong with that?"

"Like I said. Everything. Nothing," she said, sighing as she leaned into his embrace. "There's so much between us. That's why I pushed you away."

"There's good between us," he said, his tone reasonable, while his mouth was anything but. "You know that. We're good together. And I'm back. So stop pushing."

He was right. They were good together. And it was scaring her silly. "But what about all the others?"

"There doesn't have to be anything but this," he said. Then he drew his head back to give her a long, appraising look. "This is the part where I kiss you again. I just want to warn you."

"That's very considerate of you, since I told you we can't do that again."

"Yeah, I remember. You were very firm in your protests."

"I'm still firm on that matter, but I am sorry I was so abrupt and mean."

"You could never be mean. And I can't help it, Freddie. I want to kiss you."

Then he did just that, to prove his point.

It *was* good. Very good. She felt as if the night had turned into a beautiful dream. Clay's arms were strong, but undemanding. His kiss was sure, but uncomplicated. It all felt so right, so wonderful, that for a brief flicker of time, she forgot all the things that could drive them apart. She kissed him back, listening to the ocean as it breathed life into the shore, listening to the wind as it caressed the trees, listening to her own heartbeat merge with Clay's as he held her close and made her feel as if she were the only person who mattered.

Finally he lifted his head and touched his forehead to hers. "See, nothing wrong here. We…we need this."

She pulled away, reluctant now instead of resistant. "But…you brought me down here to talk, didn't you?"

He gave her that little-boy grin. "Yeah, but I kind of forgot all about that."

"That's my point exactly. We can't forget it, Clay. We can't forget that I have a past that still haunts me, that you have things on your mind."

"Yeah, well, I'm willing to sort through my problems, so I can be with you. I'm only asking that you do the same."

She put a hand to his chest. "I'm not sure I can do that."

"What if...what if I told you the truth?"

She felt panic rushing through her like a changing tide. "The truth?"

He touched a hand to her cheek. "Rock says I need to do two things—turn it all over to God, and tell you the truth about everything."

"Rock is a very smart man."

Clay nodded, nuzzled her hair with his face. "Yeah, he made me see that I'm harboring some big-time resentment toward my mother. I had to be honest with her about that. We got a lot of things cleared up. And now I have to be honest with you. But that works two ways, Freddie. I need you to be up-front with me, too."

"I've tried. I'm trying to be honest with you right now."

He stepped back, groaning. "I'm not doing this right. I brought you down here so I could bare my soul to you, and now I'm asking you to do the same. Will you just listen to me? Will you let me tell you everything?"

She saw the need in his eyes. Saw all the pain, fear and doubt she felt inside. "Okay," she said. "I'm listening."

But in her heart, Freddie knew she didn't have to listen to Clay's confessions to understand that she had fallen in love with him. That was very obvious to her now. It was also very obvious that she couldn't let him see that. She was still afraid to be completely honest. And she had no idea how to handle that.

I could use some guidance, Lord, she thought now as she looked up at Clay. What was right? What was wrong? She'd come here to escape, to start a new life, to find a better road. If she gave in to loving Clay, she'd be right back where she'd started, involved with a police officer.

But a very different man from the first one.

She thought of Gary. Thought of how handsome he was when they'd first met. Thought of how he'd worked so hard here in Georgia to find a job at a small-town police station. Remembered how he'd pursued her and how she'd fallen in love so quickly. Then she remembered how after she'd had Ryan, Gary had decided to move to Dallas to work with his brother and his father. The family together again.

But the family hadn't been a family at all. Not in the real sense of the word. They'd only been coconspirators in deception and fraud. Pearl had looked the other way for years. Freddie had been expected to do the same. She'd married into a family of bad cops. And that had cost Gary his life, and cost Freddie her soul.

She looked at Clay now, saw the good in his beautiful eyes, saw the honor and valor in his every action and deed. He wasn't a bad cop. He was a good man who'd gotten caught up in a bad situation. Freddie wanted to know the whole story, if only to convince herself that Clay was different.

But what if he had something to hide, too? What if his need to confess had something to do with his line of work?

"You're not sure about me, are you?" Clay asked her now. He tugged her down onto the moist sand, his eyes never leaving her face.

Freddie sank down beside him. "I'm not sure about life in general. I don't want to make another mistake."

Clay hung his hands over his bent knees, then stared out into the dark waters. "I know that feeling. But I also know that from the first time I saw you, something changed inside me. I don't know why…but I think God has His reasons…you know, for the way things happen."

"Then what was His reason for Gary?"

Clay shook his head. "You got me there. Gary was lost, Freddie. Lost in power and greed. I've seen it. You've seen it firsthand. I can't change that. I can only tell you that I'm sorry and that…I'm not that way. Maybe you had to know Gary…before you could know me. So you could see that there is a difference."

"Okay." She took his hand. "Tell me everything."

Clay gripped her fingers, then brought her hand to his mouth for a quick kiss. "I love being a cop," he said, the words soft and husky as they lifted out over the night wind. "I want to continue being a police officer, a K-9 officer. But Samson and me, we both suffered wounds that night. And we're both still healing."

"I know about Samson," she said, her hand tightening on his. "I want to know more about you."

He told her about how the suspect had stabbed him with the frayed, jagged rebar. Told her of the intense pain he'd felt just before he'd managed to get off a couple of shots. Then he turned to face her. "I killed a sixteen-year-old, Freddie."

Suddenly, Freddie saw everything, all the pain and doubt, all the guilt centered there in his face. "That's it, isn't it? You've healed physically, but not emotionally?"

"Something like that." He shrugged. "The stab was deep, but clean. It hurt like everything for a few weeks, but I'm fine now. Samson took a while longer, of course. But my captain was worried about my mental state. You see, I'd never…killed anyone before."

"And you killed a kid."

"Yeah, a kid. A teenager who should have been enjoying high school and football or maybe baseball or basketball, and girls. A kid who should have been planning for college and a good future. Instead, he was running drugs for some big-shot thug. It makes me sick."

"You can't control that, Clay."

"But I killed him. He'll never get a second chance."

Freddie turned to him then. "But *you* did get a second chance. You survived that night, for some reason."

"Yeah, well, I feel guilty every time I look in the mirror."

"Don't," she said. When she thought about how close he'd come to death, how she might not have ever gotten to know him, her heart shifted like a castle in the sand. Then she pulled his head into her hands. "Don't ever feel that way, Clay. You survived for a reason, don't you think?"

"I don't know. I don't know if I'm worthy of that."

"You are," Freddie told him. "You are."

Then she pulled his head toward her own and kissed him, long and hard, her lips touching on his with what she hoped was a healing power. "You are so important to a lot of people."

Clay stilled her hands on his face, his fingers gripping her wrists in midair. "I want to be important to *you,* and to Ryan. I think…I believe you can help me get through all of this and decide what to do from here on out. I'm counting on you for that, Freddie. I need you."

Freddie stared up at him, feeling the weight of his need, feeling a thousand emotions rushing over her while the ocean lapped at her feet. Did she dare give in to her own needs? Or should she tell Clay he couldn't depend on her, for anything?

"I need you," he told her again. Then he pulled her

close, kissing her until she couldn't think of anything but being in his arms.

And in her dreams, they were together like this, here on the beach, for a very long time. In her dreams, she would be with Clay forever. But in reality, her unreasonable fears took over, and forever was much too soon and much too long. Her own need seemed to overwhelm her. She couldn't do this. She had to tell Clay she couldn't do this.

Chapter Twelve

"**S**top," she said, pulling away from him. "We have to stop, now."

Clay's heart was racing at breakneck speed. He didn't want to stop. "What's wrong?" he said, a sick dread pooling inside his soul.

Freddie got up, brushing the sand off her jeans. "I'm…I'm not ready for this."

Clay pushed up to stand beside her. She looked so lost and confused, standing there in the moonlight, with the ocean behind her and the wind in her long, dark hair. "I pushed you too fast, didn't I?"

She crossed her arms, shivering, as she stared up at him. "You…you are very direct, Clay. You are also very…overwhelming."

He wanted to reach for her, to warm her, to comfort

her. But he held back. "I only go after things that I really want, Freddie."

"And you think you want me. You think that we belong together."

"Yes, that's what I think. You feel the same way, don't you?"

He could see the denial in her dark eyes. "I think," she said, turning her head so she didn't have to look at him, "I think that you're rebounding from a crisis and that I'm the first positive thing you've found since that crisis."

"That works," he said with a shrug. "You are good for me."

"But can't you see, it's like a puppy that bonds with the first human to touch him. You don't know any better."

"Are you comparing me to a dog?" he said with a brittle laugh.

"No." She gave him an amused expression, in spite of the pain in her eyes. "You know what I'm saying, though, don't you? What if what you're feeling for me is just a temporary fix? What if you go back to Atlanta next week and decide this was just an end-of-summer fling?"

He did reach for her then, tugging her close, his hands on her arms. "Don't insult me, Freddie. We've teased each other about that, but I'm not that type. We're not teenagers. This is more than just a whim. And it's certainly more than just bonding with someone. Do you think I'm that needy?"

She stared up at him, her eyes brimming with tears. "I think you need me, Clay. I think you need me to help you through this, but what happens after you're back on the force in Atlanta? Where do we go then?"

"I don't have to go back," he said, meaning it and knowing it was what he wanted in his heart. He hadn't been able to admit that until now, though. "I can stay here on the island."

"Oh, no," she replied, pulling out of his grasp. "No, you are not going to throw away your career just because you think you have feelings for me. I can't let you do that. And I don't want you to do that."

"What if I told you I'd already been considering doing that, before I even met you?"

"I don't believe you," she retorted. "You've told me how much you love your job in Atlanta."

Trying to make her see reason, Clay turned her around again. "I love being a cop. I never said I loved working in Atlanta. After all I've been through over the last few months, believe me, I'd settle for a nice, quiet patrol around the island anytime."

"You'd *settle*," she replied, her expression taut with determination and disbelief. "You'd *settle*...for a safe, boring job here, with a safe, boring woman?"

"The job might be boring, but you could never be. How could you even think that?"

She waved her hands in the air. "I can't let you do this, Clay. I can't let this happen. You need to go back to Atlanta, if for no other reason, to see if you still have what it takes to be a police officer. You're just…mixed up and hurting. You need time to think this through. And while you're thinking, leave me out of the equation. If you can honestly decide that you'd rather be a patrol officer here on the island instead of a K-9 cop back in the big city, then…then that's something you have to decide on your own. I won't be responsible for what could be the biggest mistake of your life."

He grabbed her arm. "You won't be responsible, or you don't want to be involved? Which is it, Freddie?"

"It's both," she shouted. "I've tried and tried to tell you, I can't deal with this right now. I just got settled here myself—"

"And what are *you* settling for?" he demanded, his temper getting the better of him. "Aren't you settling for a safe, boring life yourself, tucked away here from the world? Secure but alone, safe but miserable?"

"I am not miserable," she shouted, her eyes blazing. "I have my work and my son, and I intend to concentrate on both. I have to remember what brought me here in the first place. I have to remember what I left behind."

"Oh, right. You were married to a cop. Well, here's a news flash, Freddie. You need to get over that. I am truly sorry for what Gary put you through, and I'm sorry that he had to die in such a horrible way. I'm sorry that Ryan lost his father, and that you got burned so badly. But I'm not sorry that we found each other. I will not apologize for that, or for how I feel about you. And…I won't apologize for being a police officer."

She backed away, her hand going to her mouth. "After all the time we've spent together, you still can't see what I'm going through, can you?"

"I guess not," he said, his heart sinking with each step she took, "*because* of all the time we've spent together. I mean, you say one thing, when you really want something else entirely. You're fighting this for all the wrong reasons."

"I am fighting," she retorted. "I'm fighting you. I knew I'd upset you the other night, and I wanted to call you, to see you, and explain why I reacted the way I did. I thought tonight would be different, but I'm still not ready, Clay. And I am truly sorry for that. I don't have any other excuses." She shrugged, held her body erect. "Maybe…maybe we shouldn't see each other again. Even as friends."

He'd lost her, right here on the very night he'd hoped to win her over. "I guess you must be right. This isn't working." With a defeat that left him cold and numb, he threw his hands in the air. "Okay. You win. I'll go back to Atlanta. I'll do my job and concentrate on deciding what's right for me. And I won't obligate you to do anything. You're free, Freddie. Off the hook."

He took a deep breath, then said, "But I want you to

remember something my mother and I talked about. She finally admitted that after my father died, she was afraid to love her children. She was so afraid of loving us too much, so afraid of losing us the way she'd lost him, that she put a long, painful distance between us. That's a gap that's only now beginning to close." He thumped his chest with a finger. "And look at me, Freddie. I'm a grown man. And yet, that distance, that denial, cost me so much. It cost my mother, and it cost my brothers and me, so much. Don't do that to yourself and your son. Don't…turn me away because you're afraid of loving me."

He started walking back toward the boardwalk, but he pivoted when he was a few feet from her. "I'm going back, but I want you to think long and hard while I'm gone. And if you decide you want to let me love you, well, you know where to find me."

"Let's find out what the problem is," Freddie told the blond woman who stood holding the tiny, trembling Shih tzu close in her arms.

"Dr. Hayes, you have to help Misty," the woman said, her big eyes tearing up. "Something is terribly wrong."

Freddie had to agree with that statement. Something was terribly wrong in her own life, too, and she didn't even want to admit what it was.

Except that Clay was gone.

He'd left a week ago. She'd found out from talking to her friends at Ana's tearoom. He hadn't told her goodbye, but then she hadn't expected him to. They'd pretty much ended everything that night on the beach.

Because she hadn't heard from Clay since that horrible scene, she'd swallowed her pride and asked Ana about him when she'd stopped in for a quick lunch. "Have you seen Clay? I haven't talked to him in a couple of days."

Ana's eyebrows lifted. "You mean, you don't know?"

"Know what?" Freddie asked, her heart racing as all sorts of scenarios played through her head. But in her heart, she knew what Ana was going to say. Clay had told her he would leave.

"He just up and left," Jackie interjected with a sympathetic glance. "Told his mamma goodbye, went to see Rock, then took that dog and left."

Freddie could see that Ana and her friends had questions, but Ana's warning glance had ended any further discussion. "It's true," she'd added to Jackie's news. "Clay's gone back to Atlanta. I...I thought you knew."

Freddie could only stare down at her chicken-salad sandwich. "No, I...I've been so busy."

Thank goodness for Ana's discretion. Ana hadn't pushed her for explanations, but all of the women had been very quiet. Too quiet. Freddie could feel their pity and their curiosity. But she couldn't bring herself to tell them that she'd forced Clay to leave. Her appetite gone, she'd gotten up and left.

"What are we going to do?" the woman now asked Freddie, bringing her back to the tiny bundle of yelping dog.

"Let me try to examine her, Mrs. Kimberly," Freddie said to the frightened woman. She'd already tried to take the little dog once, but Misty kept snapping and snarling. "It's certainly not like Misty to be afraid of me."

"No, that's just it," Mrs. Kimberly said, shaking her head. "Misty loves you. But this morning, she wouldn't even let me put her up on the bed with me. She snapped at me every time I tried to lift her."

With a gentle tug, Freddie extracted the fluffy dog from Mrs. Kimberly, careful to avoid Misty's sharp little teeth. "Lee," Freddie called, "I need some help."

Kate came rushing in. "Lee's got a crisis in the waiting room, Dr. Hayes. Bertha Sledge had to leave her cat with us because she thinks Tinker is about to have her kittens, but Bertha was late for an appointment and couldn't stay. We took Tinker to an exam room, but somehow, Tinker got away from Lee and ran back into the waiting room. Now Tinker is giving birth to her kittens in the corner by the toy box, and she won't let anyone near her to help her."

"Oh, my," Mrs. Kimberly said, her mouth opening wide. "Do you always have this much excitement around here?"

"No, not normally," Freddie said as she and Kate held Misty down on the examining table. "It's usually pretty boring around here."

Boring.

Had she settled for a boring life here on the island? Granted, there was plenty to do and see. And she'd made lots of new friends. She'd even found her faith again. But what about love? What about a soul mate? What about the kind of life she'd always hoped to have when she'd married Gary? Was she willing to forgo all of that simply because she'd made bad choices the first time around? Was she throwing away a second chance, her one chance to find the kind of deep, abiding love that only a solid marriage could bring?

You saw that with your parents, she reminded herself as her fingers deftly moved over Misty's trembling body. They'd had a real love, based on faith and respect for each other. Freddie only wanted the same.

You could have that with Clay.

But Clay's gone now.

"Ouch!" Kate's peal of pain caused Freddie to glance up. "Misty, you bit me," the girl said, shock in her voice as she stared down at the fierce little animal. "What's the matter, baby?" Then seeing Mrs. Kimberly's obvious dismay, she quickly added, "It's just a nip. Hardly broke the skin on my finger."

"I think I've found the problem," Freddie said, a smile breaking through the gloom in her mind. "Misty seems to have gotten a burr on her belly. That's why she cried out each time you tried to pick her up, Mrs. Kimberly." Patting the little dog on the head, Freddie added, "And that's why she bit you, Kate. She's just trying to protect herself."

"My baby has a burr in her bonnet," Mrs. Kimberly said, cooing down at Misty.

A burr in her bonnet. Maybe that's what I have, too, Freddie thought with a grim realization. She was trying to protect herself from the pain. And each time someone reached out to help her, she snapped and lashed out.

She'd done that to Clay. She'd deliberately lashed out at the one man who could give her the kind of stability and love she'd always craved. A good love, based on faith and family, honor and integrity.

A good love that she'd thrown away because of fear and pain.

"Got it," Freddie said as she gently extracted the round, thorn-covered sticker from Misty's thick fur. The little dog immediately stopped struggling and settled down, looking up at Freddie with dark, watery eyes. But those eyes were once again filled with trust. Freddie had taken the pain away.

Trust. Suddenly, Freddie understood. She had to stop struggling and trust in God and in Clay. It was the only way to get rid of the pain in her soul. And it had taken a little muff with a thorn in her side to teach Freddie that lesson. Rock was so right. God did indeed work in mysterious ways.

Freddie glanced up, a smile on her face in spite of the tears forming in her eyes. Kate stared across at her. "Are you all right, Doc?"

Freddie blinked, smiled, fell back on her old reliable excuse. "Sorry. I just hate to see an animal in pain."

And I've realized I love Clay Dempsey, she wanted to shout. But more importantly, she'd realized she *could* love Clay. She could let go of the pain, and let Clay's love and God's power heal her. She just had to stop struggling.

"You are a very good doctor," Mrs. Kimberly said. She reached across the table and hugged Freddie. "I'm going to say a special prayer for you, my friend."

"I'll need that prayer," Freddie said, gratitude filling her heart with joy. After making sure Misty was indeed okay, she turned to Kate. "Take care of that nip on your finger, then we'd better go check on that mother cat."

As they ushered Mrs. Kimberly and tiny Misty out of the room, Lee called out, "The babies are coming, Doc. You'd better hurry in here."

Freddie rushed into the waiting room to find Lee crouching down in the corner while four curious humans, an iguana, two yelping dogs—one a huge Great Dane and the other a long-bodied dachshund—and yet another meowing cat, watched the entire birth.

"Such a wonder," one woman said, patting the carrying cage of her own cat.

It was a wonder, Freddie thought. Life was truly a gift and a wonder. She wished she hadn't waited so long to discover that.

"You're sure gonna be tired tonight," Lee said over his shoulder to her. "But not as tired as this little mama."

"I'll get the other patients to their rooms," Kate said, waving toward the teenager with the iguana. "David, bring Icky to room three. What a day."

In a matter of minutes, the area was cleared and Freddie was left to the task of watching over the scared mama cat while she delivered her kittens.

"Let me see about her, Lee," Freddie said as she sank down onto the floor, everything in her world now bright and clear. She wanted to laugh. She wanted to cry. But most of all, she wanted to find Clay and tell him that she loved him. If it wasn't too late.

Lord, please don't let it be too late.

Glancing up at the clock, she saw that it was almost time to go get Ryan from school. But she couldn't leave the mother cat and the kittens, nor her other patients. Turning to find Kate back at the desk, Freddie called out to her. "Kate, could you possibly go and get Ryan from school for me? I didn't realize it was so late."

Kate glanced at the clock, too. "Oh, Doc, I have a class in an hour. I'm going to be pushing it just to get there on time. And we have an exam today."

"Go then," Freddie said, her hand stroking the back

of the frightened mother cat. "I forgot you needed to leave early." Who could she call?

"I'll go get the boy for you," Lee offered, his hands on his hips. "All of the other patients are settled for now. They don't mind waiting, and…it's only around the block. I'll be back in two shakes of a monkey's tail."

Freddie hesitated, remembering how Lee had coaxed Ryan with an ice cream on the boardwalk. But he'd apologized for that. And since then, he'd been nothing but kind to both Freddie and Ryan. Everyone on the island vouched for Lee, even Rock. Rock had assured her that Lee was a steady Christian, just a Christian who marched to the beat of a different drummer. He was a dependable, eccentric beach bum, but he'd proven his merit time and again. And the school was a short walk down the road, with teachers watching and a patrol at the crosswalk.

Trust. She had to learn to trust.

"Okay, if you don't mind," she said just as the cat went into another round of contractions. "I'd appreciate that, Lee. First, call the school, so I can tell them you're coming to get Ryan and that it's okay. You'll have to bring the phone to me. They'll need to get my approval."

Lee did as she had asked. After the school secretary had assured her they'd make sure Ryan left with Lee, Freddie turned back to the task at hand, her mind still on Clay.

She had to call Clay tonight.
To tell him that they needed to talk.
About their future.

Chapter Thirteen

Freddie knew something was wrong. It had been a half hour since Lee had left to go get Ryan.

After the first ten minutes, she'd called the school and the secretary had told her that Ryan had left with Lee. "I watched them myself until they'd walked all the way down to the corner toward the clinic. They should be walking in any minute now, Mrs. Hayes."

They hadn't made it yet. Freddie had delivered the five kittens, then gotten through one quick exam and sent that animal away with flea protection, then hurriedly explained to the remaining patients that she had a personal emergency and they'd have to reschedule. No one had argued with her.

"Don't panic," she told herself as she hurried to lock up, making sure the new mama cat and her babies were secure in a clean cage. Lee had probably stopped for ice cream again.

Why did I let him go? she wondered now as she rushed out the front door. She'd tried to be so careful, so protective. Why hadn't she just stopped everything to go get Ryan herself?

Because you were distracted by too many patients. And by Clay Dempsey.

She'd been thinking of Clay. She'd been thinking only of how much she wanted to talk to Clay.

As she stepped outside, she took a deep breath, telling herself everything would be all right. The school staff knew Lee. There were witnesses who'd watched him walking with Ryan. Surely Lee wouldn't be so stupid—it was only a few yards from the corner to the clinic. But no one would have been able to see Ryan and Lee from the school after they'd rounded the corner. A few short yards, with no one around and her too busy inside the clinic to be watching.

Freddie's panic set in full force as she ran up the sidewalk toward the school. She saw other mothers with their children, but she didn't see Lee and Ryan.

Frantic and out of breath, she ran into the school. "Where's Ryan?" she asked the first teacher she saw.

"Hi, Mrs. Hayes. What's wrong?" the woman asked, holding Freddie still when she saw Freddie's scared expression.

"Ryan. He hasn't made it home. Lee Fletcher came to get him. I gave my consent."

"Oh, of course," the woman said, her eyes full of understanding. "Lee did pick up Ryan. They were headed back to the clinic last time I saw them. Everything seemed fine."

"Everything is not fine!" Freddie said, fear filling her throat with a sickening bile. "I have to find my son."

The woman went into action, calling out for the principal and all the teachers who'd been on duty outside the school. Soon, they were all searching around the parking lot and down the block. The principal convinced Freddie to go wait at the clinic, and wisely sent an aide to sit with her. Freddie called Ryan's name all the way back to the clinic, but Ryan was nowhere to be found.

And she couldn't sit. She now paced the sidewalk, her eyes on the empty, quiet street. She held her cell phone in her hand, helpless as to who to call. The school had already called the island patrol, just as a precaution. And she had no one else. Clay came to mind. Clay would know exactly what to do. But Freddie couldn't call him now. He was too far away. And she was standing here alone on the sidewalk, wondering where her son was.

Ryan. Her mind shouted his name, her mother's heart falling apart piece by piece. She was going to be sick. She wanted to run down the street screaming. She wanted to turn back the clock. She wanted her son here safe. Thinking back over the day, Freddie wondered why she'd even considered letting someone else go get Ryan. She always scheduled a block of free time after school—a quick ten-minute walk around the corner and back. But today, she'd been so busy, so preoccupied. Too much happening at once.

"How could I have been so stupid?" she said out loud, causing the worried aide at her side to look up at her.

"I'm sure it will be all right, Mrs. Hayes," the young woman said, but she didn't seem convinced herself from what Freddie could tell.

When a van pulled up, Freddie glanced around with hope, only to find Rock coming toward her, a concerned expression on his face. "One of the teachers called me," he said as he came up to Freddie. "She thought you might need me here."

"Why?" Freddie asked, panic causing the one word to turn into a moan. "Oh, Rock, don't tell me—"

"I don't have any information," Rock said, grabbing her to get her attention. "I'm just here to help. I don't have any news, Freddie. I'm sorry."

"I knew better," she said, the tears forming in her eyes now, hot and heavy and sickening. "I should have gone myself. We were so busy and Kate had to leave early. I was so…I had to get the patients out, and every-body kept telling me Lee was safe, reliable—that he wouldn't hurt Ryan." *And I was distracted.*

She thought of Clay and the joy she'd felt at finally accepting that she loved him. But that joy was now tainted with a new, gripping fear. "Oh, Rock, what have I done?"

She fell into his arms. Rock held her close, his words soft and soothing. "It's going to be all right, Freddie. Lee Fletcher *wouldn't* hurt a fly. It's going to be all right. I'm sure they're just off doing something fun. You know Lee is considered very cool by all the local kids. He wouldn't harm any of them. You have to believe that."

"Why did I let him go get Ryan?" Freddie asked, not even hearing Rock's assurances. She pulled away, turned. "I have to go. I have to do something. I can't just stand here."

When she looked up to find the familiar island-patrol SUV coming down the street, her knees gave out and she sank down onto the ground. "No, no. This can't be happening. Why didn't I just go get my son myself?"

Rock sat down beside her, his hands on her arms as he stared into her eyes. "We'll find him, Freddie. I promise."

Freddie knew all about promises. She knew all about being disappointed. And she knew that if something had happened to her son, it was all her fault.

It had been two hours. Two hours of sheer, gut-wrenching agony. And now, a storm was brewing outside, the sky dark, ominous and scurrying, the lightning clashing in angry shards of pure fire that hurt Freddie's eyes, the thunder marching closer and closer with a booming, mocking accuracy. Freddie wanted to curl up in a ball and disappear into herself. She wanted to hold Ryan close in her arms and never let him go. She'd made a terrible mistake and now her son was paying for that mistake.

She felt a hand on her arm and looked up from her spot by the cottage window to find Ana offering her yet another cup of hot tea. "I can't," Freddie said, shaking her head.

Wasn't it enough that they'd insisted she come home to wait? Wasn't it enough that they'd left someone standing guard at the clinic in case Ryan showed up there? Wasn't it enough that she'd let her guard down just once and now she was paying for that with every fiber of her being? She didn't want tea or food. She wanted to be left alone. She wanted her son back, back from that cold, wet scary world out there. Back from this nightmare that wouldn't end.

Ana silently set the cup down on the table beside Freddie's chair, then settled herself in the matching chair across from the table. She didn't speak, just sat there with her hands folded, her expression etched with quiet concern. The seconds ticked by, uncaring and unrelenting, while Freddie, unable to look at Ana, watched the clock on the wall, then turned to stare out the window again.

And then Ana said, "I called Clay."

Freddie pivoted from the window, shock coursing like cold water through her body. "You did what?"

"I called Clay," Ana said, her defiant chin coming up. "They've put out a missing-child alert bulletin, and everyone is searching. But you need Clay here. And Samson."

Freddie remembered Clay's words about his job. "Search and rescue. Or sometimes, just search and find." As in, a dead body.

She jumped up and rushed down the hall to the bathroom, where she became violently ill. Ana was right there with a cool, clean rag. She held Freddie as she slowly tried to stand up. After helping Freddie rinse her mouth and face, Ana said, "Let me get you to your bed."

Freddie couldn't speak, couldn't get past putting one foot in front of the other. Her skin felt clammy with fever, but she was cold, so cold. Her son was gone, gone. Missing. And it was her fault. Her stupid fault. All of her careful plans, her security system and self-defense lessons hadn't helped one bit in the end. She couldn't help her son now and it was killing her. She wanted to die. Instead, she fell across the bed, and allowed Ana to cover her with a sunflower-splashed afghan.

BoBo hopped up on the bed, his cute kitten face expectant and playful. The little cat only made Freddie that much more aware of her missing son. Ryan loved BoBo. The kitten meowed, as if asking her what was wrong. Freddie grabbed the tiny cat and held him close, breathing in the warm sweet scent of him.

"Do you need anything?" Ana asked, her voice like a soft song lifting through the total blackness of Freddie's dark despair.

I need my son back. But she couldn't say that, because to voice it might mean the worst. But Ana had called Clay. Clay. And Samson. Thinking of that big, lovable, dependable dog caused a dam of pain and longing to burst forth in Freddie's shocked system.

She grabbed Ana's hand, sobs racking her body. "Thank you," she finally managed to get out. "Thank you."

She knew what she needed, just as Ana had. She needed Clay here. But she also knew that they could never be together now. She'd lost her son almost simultaneously with discovering she could love again. And it was too late. Her heart was shattered into a million crystal-hard pieces. She had no more room for love.

But the need inside her soul cried out for that love.

God, dear God, help me, she silently screamed. *Help me, dear Father. Help my son. Protect him. Bring him back to me. Please, God.*

If she could just have that one prayer answered, she could learn to live without any of the rest. She'd pour all of her love on her son, if God would just bring him back to her. That had been her original plan.

That should have been enough.

That would have to be enough.

If only God would listen to her prayers.

* * *

He prayed. Clay pushed his truck up the highway, hoping he'd make it to the island before the storm hit, his mind reeling between prayers and plans.

He had to find Ryan. Samson wouldn't let him down.

Clay glanced over at the big dog. Samson knew something was up. The animal sat alert and watchful, his big eyes turning to Clay with a questioning trust.

"We'll find him, won't we, buddy?"

Samson barked an affirmative, his tongue hanging out in anticipation. He was ready to do his job.

Clay prayed they could both do their job.

He still felt a shudder of apprehension as he recalled Ana's words to him over the phone hours before. "You need to come home, Clay. Something's happened. Ryan Hayes is missing."

Clay's instincts told him that Uncle Todd had something to do with this. He couldn't believe gentle, laid-back Lee Fletcher would kidnap or harm a child. It just wasn't in Lee's nature. Clay's best guess was that this was the work of Todd Hayes.

And if that was the case, then all the careful preparations Clay had helped Freddie with didn't matter one bit. Because a cop would know how to get around those preparations, those precautions. And a bad cop, well, a bad cop would also be more than willing to go around the law and everything in-between, just to get what he wanted.

In this case, an innocent little boy.

Clay prayed. And while he prayed, he accepted that he loved Freddie Hayes and her son, Ryan. While he prayed, he vowed he would find Ryan and he would make that little boy's mother happy and secure, because he loved her. But if she couldn't accept that, then finding Ryan would have to be enough.

It had to be enough. He wanted to bring Ryan back and he wanted to bring Freddie's heart out of its shell. But he might not get both of those wishes.

Dear Lord, help me to get that child back safely to his mother. That's all I ask now, Lord. Help me. Help all of us. And please, keep Ryan safe.

He was almost home. He would soon be there with Freddie. He didn't intend to leave Sunset Island again until he'd found Ryan, because if something had happened to that boy, Freddie's heart would shut down for good. And she'd never accept any promises again. Not from Clay. And not from God.

She heard a knocking. It sounded so faraway and distant. It was a gentle knocking, a soft tapping that sounded as if someone wanted to get in, but didn't want to bother her. She wasn't really asleep, but she was obviously dreaming. She thought she heard a voice, a gentle, calm voice.

"Do you hear me, Freddie? Let me in."

In her dream, Freddie felt a comforting hand on her shoulder. She thought she saw Christ there beside her,

His hand held out to her, His silhouette shining with a muted, glowing light. "Let me in, Freddie."

Freddie tried to reach for His hand. She wanted the comfort only He could bring.

The knocking brought her fully awake.

And then she remembered. Ryan was missing. Ryan was missing and she'd almost fallen asleep. With a frantic need, she jumped up and ran through the house toward the front door. Ana was there, opening it. There were several other people in the room, but Freddie couldn't seem to focus on all the familiar faces. It was raining and the wind pushed at the door, sending it back on its hinges.

Samson bounded into the house and headed down the hall toward Ryan's room, his bark anxious and playful. Somewhere in the back of the house, she heard the hiss of a cat. Clay stood there, drenched and dark, his eyes searching her face, his expression carved in pain and sympathy.

Freddie gasped, brought her hands to her mouth. She couldn't seem to move. She thought she might be sick again, thought she might faint and go back into that fitful half sleep that protected her from this reality, this horror. This knife-edged need that caused her knees to buckle.

Clay didn't speak. He just came into the room and scooped her up in his arms. Parting the crowd gathered around, he took her to the chair by the window and pulled her close onto his lap, his arms moving over her shoulders with an assuring strength. Ana produced a chenille throw. Clay took it and put it over Freddie's shaking body, then he tucked her head into the crook of his arms.

"It's going to be all right now, I promise. I'm going to find him, Freddie. Do you hear me? I'm going to find your son."

She felt his kiss on the top of her head, felt the warmth of his big, strong body fighting through his damp clothes, felt the beat of his heart, so steady, so sure, as he held her there in his arms. For a while he didn't speak; he just held her, his arms moving up and down her back, his chin touching on her head.

Freddie clung to him, took in the warmth of his protection, accepted that she needed him tonight. She remembered her half dream, remembered Christ standing there beside her. "It's me, Freddie. Let me in."

Freddie closed her eyes as silent tears fell down her face. She wanted to let them both in—both Clay and the Lord. But her heart was so hurt. Her soul was so bruised. She was so afraid.

She tried to whisper. Clay heard her and held her head up with a gentle hand, his misty sea-colored gaze anchoring her fears. "What, baby?"

"Don't leave me," she said, then she buried her head against his chest and cried. *Don't leave me, Lord,* she said over and over again in her silent, screaming mind.

Don't leave me. Please don't leave my little boy out there all alone.

"I'm not going anywhere," Clay told her. "Do you hear me, Freddie?"

She managed a nod. "Find my son."

"I will," Clay promised. "Samson and I will do that. You don't have to worry anymore."

But she did worry. How could she not worry?

She felt reassured, just having Clay here. But in that little black opening in the back of her soul, she could hear that silent scream pushing through.

What if it was too late?

Chapter Fourteen

"We've searched every inch of this island," Chief Ed Anderson told Clay around midnight. "Lee and that boy have just disappeared. And on foot, too, since Lee doesn't even own a car."

"Which means they could be hiding somewhere." Not wanting to think about the implications of that, Clay decided he was going to have to bypass old Chief Anderson and do things his way. In spite of the Chief's obvious concern and compassion, Clay didn't think the man was moving things along fast enough. "Samson and I are going out for a hasty search, Chief."

The ruddy-faced officer shot Clay a tired, doubtful look. "I told you—I've called for reinforcements from Savannah. We'll start fresh in the morning with volunteers and professionals with tracking hounds, after this rain has died down—"

Clay held up a hand. "And I've told you, I'm not waiting another minute. You know how critical the first twenty-fours hours are, Chief. I've set up a command post at the church and I'm going back out there tonight. I've got volunteers waiting, and I've got a trained search dog ready to get to work."

"This ain't your jurisdiction," the chief reminded him.

"I'm not going to argue over the details," Clay retorted. "We can talk command posts and search grids tomorrow, but right now, every minute counts. I'm just going to let Samson do his job."

"Yeah, well, good luck to you, boy."

Clay left the patrol station, thinking he needed luck. And prayers. Rock had been right there by his side, doing whatever Clay asked, while Ana, Eloise and several other women, some of them officers' wives, had stayed behind with Freddie at her cottage. And Miss McPherson, bless her, had opened her home to the volunteers, serving them hot drinks, sandwiches and homemade brownies. The whole island was out and about, everyone willing to help find Ryan.

Right now, Rock was with Kate back at the clinic, supervising while two part-time officers, working on their own time now, went over the place with a fine-tooth comb. They planned to interview everyone who'd been at the clinic, too. Hopefully, somebody had seen something.

At least Chief Anderson had some men search Lee's tiny beach hut. They'd found nothing amiss there. Lee might be a bum, but he was a tidy bum. And a clean one, suspectwise. He had a clear record, not even a misdemeanor or traffic violation. Nothing to reveal why he might have taken Ryan. The man didn't even own a phone or a computer. All they'd found were stacks of books, some poetry journals, and some day-old pizza in the refrigerator. The books were mostly classic literature and fishing magazines, and the poetry journals only revealed that Lee had a bent toward bad rhymes. Nothing in there about wanting to take a child away from his mother.

Samson had nosed around the three-room apartment, taking in the scents. Clay had allowed Samson to get a good whiff of one of Lee's dirty shirts piled in a basket beside the tiny combined washer-dryer unit in the small kitchen. If they could find Lee, surely they'd find Ryan, too.

Now, the shirt safe in a plastic Ziploc bag on the seat of his truck, Clay headed back to the clinic to begin the search from square one, glad that the storm had turned into a drizzle. It would be tough finding anybody in this black void, but he was determined to keep looking. Samson was eager to get started. And Samson was well trained for this type of search. Clay just hoped the dog was up to the search physically. Samson would push to the limit if Clay demanded it of him.

Clay was beyond anxious. His heart hurt each time he thought about the anguish in Freddie's face when she'd seen him standing at her door. He'd never forget that face. It had torn at his gut, making him feel helpless. He'd never forget the way she'd clung to him. He was her last hope. He and Samson. He couldn't let her down. And he surely wasn't going to let Ryan down.

Clay thought about how Samson had come back up the hallway from Ryan's room, his big eyes loaded with questions the animal couldn't voice. "Where's Ryan?" Samson seemed to say. Clay couldn't answer his partner's silent question.

He remembered Freddie finally pushing out of his arms, a new resolve born out of her tears and fragility. "Don't just sit here. I'm okay. I'll be okay now. Go and find him."

She'd sunk down onto the floor, her arms going around Samson's neck, her hands gripping his thick fur. "You love my Ryan, don't you, boy? You're going to find him for me, right, Samson?" Clay had heard the hitch in her voice as she hoarsely repeated the plea. "Samson, please find Ryan for me."

Samson had barked his assurances, giving her a wet kiss on the cheek, the salt of her tears alerting the dog to what was ahead.

"Almost time, boy," Clay told his companion. "We've got work to do."

Samson jumped out of the truck right behind Clay, his bark indicating he was up to the task.

* * *

They'd traced Lee's scent from the school and back in a careful grid that indicated Lee and Ryan had back-tracked almost all the way back to the clinic. It hadn't taken Samson long to alert right past the corner where the road turned to the left toward the clinic. The dog left the sidewalk, stopped on the street, barked, then started whining, almost as if he wanted to go off in another direction.

Clay turned to Chief Anderson and Rock, his gut telling him something wasn't right. "Samson doesn't want to go back to the clinic. He hesitated here when we began the search, and now he's alerting here again."

"What's that mean?" Chief Anderson asked, adjusting the plastic-covered brim of his rain hat even though the rain had stopped.

"It means the scent has changed or gotten lost," Clay said, his gaze scanning the street. "That can only mean one thing. They got into a vehicle right about here."

Rock glanced over at him. "You mean, they voluntarily got into a car?"

"If Lee had someone working with him," Clay said, the grim facts glaring him in the face. "Or—"

"Or they were forced into a car," the chief finished for him. He grunted and shifted his feet on the wet street. "Who would do such a thing?"

Clay knew exactly who. "I think the boy's uncle might have taken him."

Rock's head came up. "What are you talking about?"

Clay quickly explained how Todd Hayes had been threatening Freddie. "She was afraid of him. That's why she had that elaborate security alarm installed at the cottage. She was very careful about being at the school on time to pick up Ryan, too. But lately, the uncle had backed off."

Rock nodded. "Giving Freddie the impression she could relax a little bit."

"Exactly," Clay said, beating his fist in his hand. "He's probably been here on the island, watching and waiting for the right opportunity." *Right under my nose.* It didn't help to think that if he hadn't been so stubborn, if he'd stayed here a few more days, this might have been avoided.

"But what about Lee?" Rock asked, bringing Clay out of his self-blame. "He'd never let someone take Ryan."

"Maybe he didn't have a choice," Clay said, trying to envision the scenario in his head. "Maybe Lee didn't want to let Ryan go *by himself.* Maybe Lee had to go with them, to protect Ryan, or he was forced into the car."

"That's a lot of maybes, son," Chief Anderson said.

"Right now, that's all I've got," Clay retorted, frustration and urgency coloring his words. "We have to find Lee."

"Should we tell Freddie?" Rock asked.

"We need to question Freddie," Clay replied. "We have to find out if she's had any contact with Todd Hayes over the last few days. But first, let's just let Samson do his job. Maybe he can lead us to some more clues, at least."

"It's a start," Chief Anderson said. "Sorry I doubted you earlier, son."

"Let's go," Clay responded, giving Samson the "Go Find" command as he unfurled the dog's long leash. "Just follow us in the truck. If I have to walk every inch of this island, I'm going to find something or somebody tonight."

An hour later, Clay found someone.

Samson brought them to the end of an oyster-shell alley behind an old warehouse. Almost immediately, Samson had given a silent alert a foot away from a rusted-out old blue sedan. The car was parked under a lean-to right near the building, as if it belonged there. No one would have thought about searching it when they'd first put out the alert. Or maybe it hadn't been there earlier.

Waving to the chief and Rock to stand back, Clay waited until Anderson had eased his vehicle to a stop about fifty yards away. The men silently exited and headed toward Clay and Samson.

"Stay back," Clay told Rock in a whisper as he and Chief Anderson drew their weapons and proceeded toward the still car. Samson stood stark and unmoving, a low growl emitting from his throat.

"Anybody in there?" With quick efficiency, Clay circled the vehicle, his eyes scanning the dark interior as he beamed his flashlight inside. "It's empty," he called out to Rock.

Chief Anderson grunted and stomped, his flashlight making busy beams that hit the shadows around the car. "Nothing. A false alarm."

"Samson doesn't make false alerts," Clay told the other officer. "He brought us here for a reason."

Then they heard a tapping noise. As Clay held his gun steady and stepped closer to the car, the noise became more distinct and loud. It was followed by a muffled wail.

"In the trunk," Chief Anderson said as he rushed to the car. After doing a hasty search of the inside of the car, he stood up. "No keys. Rock, look in the back of my truck, in my toolbox, and bring me that Hurst tool. Let's see who's in there."

Rock ran to the truck, then quickly returned with the mini jaws-of-life cutter. Chief Anderson held it to the trunk, then nodded toward Clay.

Clay held his weapon drawn, then called out. "Police. Don't move. We're going to open the trunk."

Another muffled cry gave him the answer he needed.

With a bit of effort and the strength from his massive forearms, Chief Anderson popped the creaky, rusty trunk open then threw aside the cutter. He aimed his flashlight inside while Clay held his gun high. What they saw inside made them all hurry into action, including Rock.

"Lee," Clay said, relief and anguish rushing like twin rivers through his system as he pulled the man up.

"He hit me over the head," Lee said, the words bubbling out of him like spent air just as Clay removed the duct tape from his mouth. "That madman hit me on the head and…he took Ryan. He took Ryan."

"Okay, start from the beginning," Clay told Lee a few minutes later, impatience and urgency making him want to hit something himself. They'd called for backup and for the paramedics. Now Lee was sitting in the back of the ambulance, a hand to his bandaged head, while the authorities went over the car.

"I went to get Ryan," Lee said, taking long breaths as he spoke, his voice hoarse and scratchy. "Everything was just fine. We'd waved one last time to the teachers watching us, then turned back toward the clinic. A car— that car—came up kinda slow. At first, I just ignored the man, but then Ryan broke out in a grin and ran toward the car. I tried to call him back, but he seemed to know the driver. I went up to the car with Ryan, you know, just in case."

Clay listened, the pulse in his jaw quickening with a solid anger. "Then what happened, Lee?"

"The man told Ryan to get in. They'd go for a ride." He shook his head, then gripped it with a grimace. "I went up to the car and told the man, no sir, Ryan can't go anywhere without his mother's permission. I tried to pull Ryan away, but he started crying, saying that was his uncle Todd. I asked the man if that was true. He said, yes, he was Ryan's uncle." Lee stopped, held his breath, then he looked up at Clay. "That's when he nodded his head toward the seat, and I saw a big gun lying there. I asked him what he wanted. He said he only wanted to visit with his nephew. Then he told me that if I didn't like it, he'd make me wish I had. He put a hand on the gun."

Clay watched as Lee frowned and held his head. "What did you do?"

"I told him, let me go and get his mother. He said no, then he took the gun in his right hand, so Ryan couldn't see, and he patted it. He said, just keep walking. I said no, I wasn't going anywhere without Ryan." Lee slumped over, holding his head in his hands. "It was a matter of seconds, seconds. I looked around for help, but nobody was anywhere to be found and I was so worried about Ryan. He told Ryan to get in the car, that I was a bad man. Ryan looked so scared. He opened the back car door, but before they took off, Ryan dropped his backpack and had to lean down to get it. I grabbed the backpack and jumped in with Ryan."

Clay could see Lee's hands shaking. "It's okay. You did the right thing, Lee. What happened next?"

"That Hayes fellow took off. He told me if I tried anything he'd shoot me. Ryan started crying. It was bad. We drove real fast almost to the main road off the island. I knew, Clay. I knew if he got on that road, we might not ever see Ryan again."

"But Hayes brought the car here? Why'd he do that?"

"It started smoking and sputtering," Lee replied, wide-eyed. "Thank goodness for that at least. Look at the thing. It's a real clunker." He shook his head again. "The Lord was looking after us, I reckon. Hayes had to turn off the main road so he could take a look at the car. He told me and Ryan to stay inside. He waved that gun around. While he was looking under the hood, I told Ryan we had to get away. But he just kept saying Uncle Todd would take care of us." He shrugged, struggled with his words. "I couldn't tell the boy his uncle Todd was the bad one. And I was afraid something would happen to Ryan if I tried anything. So I just sat there, hoping someone would notice us."

"But no one came along?"

"No, not a soul. It's kinda deserted around this old building. Anyway, he cursed and kicked, then he got back in and tried to crank the car. It wouldn't budge. That's when he made us get out. He opened the trunk and told me to get in. Ryan started crying all over again. That made the uncle all hot and bothered. Next thing I knew, he whacked me over the head. I woke up in the trunk with my mouth taped shut, hot and thirsty and worried sick about Ryan." He looked up then. "Clay, tell me that boy's all right."

Clay had to look away. "We haven't found Ryan yet, Lee. Do you think they set out on foot?"

"Maybe," Lee said, emotion making his words thick. "Or…he coulda taken another car."

"You mean, he might have stolen another vehicle?"

"Yeah. Maybe. I don't know. I was out cold. I'm sorry."

Clay touched a hand to the man's arm. "It's all right. If they're still on this island, we'll find them. You did everything you could to protect Ryan. I won't forget that."

"What about Doc Hayes?" Lee asked, jumping up. "I have to go to her, explain what happened."

"We'll do that later," Clay told him, dreading having to relay the latest developments to Freddie. "You need to get to the hospital."

"I'm fine," Lee said, pacing in a small circle. "I want to see Dr. Hayes."

"Okay, then," Clay said. "We've got to get moving on trying to find Ryan, but I have to let her know what's happening. We'll call her, then get you to her place and you can stay there while we finish the search."

He turned to Chief Anderson. The other man nodded. "I'm on it. Got men and volunteers spreading out across the island. We're checking any reports on stolen or missing vehicles, too. Still got the main road to Savannah blocked off. He won't get far."

"It's been hours," Clay said. "Where could he have taken Ryan?" He turned back to Lee. "Think back— what did Ryan and his uncle talk about?"

Lee squinted, shrugged, paced. "Ryan was real happy to see the man, I'll tell you that. His words were falling all over themselves just to get out of his mouth— talking about the beach and dolphins and fishing and—"

Clay clutched Lee's arm. "And?"

Lee's head shot up then. "Hey, Clay, I just remembered something."

"Yeah, what?" Clay said, hope surging through him.

"The boy went on and on about the lighthouse when they first started talking. Said it was closed 'cause it was being fixed up. Said he couldn't wait to show it to his uncle. But then, things got intense and well, we forgot all about the sights. You think maybe—"

"It's a start," Clay said, turning to Chief Anderson. "Just as soon as I give Freddie an update, we can head back out, Chief. Toward the lighthouse."

Rock hurried up. "I just talked to Ana. Freddie's on her way here, Clay. Ana couldn't stop her, so she's coming with her. They heard about…the situation when one of the officers called his wife there at Freddie's house."

Clay hit his fist on the ambulance door. "Freddie doesn't need to be here."

Rock looked grim. "You mean if—"

"She just doesn't need to be here," Clay repeated.

But it was too late. He saw a car coming up the alley, going at breakneck speed. The car slid to a screeching halt and Freddie jumped out, not even bothering to shut the door. Ana was right behind her. She hurried to Rock's side while Freddie ran up to Clay.

"Where's Ryan?" she said, advancing toward Clay with a mother's fear and rage in her eyes. Then she grabbed Lee. "Where's my son?"

"I tried to save him, Doc," Lee said, tears misting in his eyes. "I tried to help him."

"Where *is* he?" Freddie cried, her hands still clutching Lee's shirt.

"We don't know," Clay told her, taking her by the arms to calm her. "Freddie, listen to me. Listen very carefully."

She managed a nod, her eyes bright, her breath coming in little spasms.

"Todd Hayes has Ryan," Clay said. He felt her body tense, saw the horror in her eyes.

"No," she said, the one word a plea. She slumped toward him. "No, Clay. He can't do this. He can't take Ryan. Tell me you won't let him do this."

"We're going after him right now," Clay said, his eyes locking with hers, his hands gripping her arms.

"Do you understand me? We think he's on foot, and he might still be on the island."

"And if he's not here?" Freddie asked, her face pale in the scattered moonlight as she pushed at him.

"We'll find him," Clay promised. "We won't stop until we do."

Freddie didn't cry this time. She didn't move. She just stood there, her eyes locked with Clay's. "He can't do this. I...I should have been more careful. I should have been watching—"

She stopped, pulled away as if he'd burned her.

Clay felt the distance between them, felt her drifting away in a cloud of despair and guilt. "We've got to go, Freddie," he said, filing the pain of her resistance and her horror back into a safe compartment for now. "We've got to go."

"I'm going with you," she said, whirling, daring him to tell her no.

"That's not a good idea—"

"I'm going," she repeated. "I can't stay in that house, doing nothing, Clay." She held a hand in the air, her finger pointed to the heavens. "That's my son out there. He's gone. None of my other tactics protected him, but I'm going to find him. Don't try to stop me."

Clay couldn't argue with her. She'd emerged out of her numb, shocked fear to become a warrior woman, willing to fight for her son. Clay loved her for it, but he was also afraid for her, too. And yet, he knew how she felt.

"Okay," he said. "But stay out of the way and do exactly as I say, you hear me?"

Freddie nodded then pushed at her damp hair. "I understand. What's the plan?"

Chapter Fifteen

"We're going to do a quick search tonight, with Samson," Clay told Freddie minutes later. "If...if we don't find anything, we'll have more search units out here first thing in the morning. We might have to bring in some bloodhounds."

Freddie couldn't, wouldn't, think past right now. "Let's go then."

Clay put a hand on her arm. His touch was tender but firm, making Freddie want to fall into his arms and let him hold her until this nightmare was over. But she resisted that urge. Her feelings for Clay were part of the reason she was standing here tonight, part of the reason her son was missing. A sick dread made her pull away from Clay's touch. He didn't try to stop her.

"You have to stay back, Freddie. Don't do anything that could put Ryan in danger, do you understand?"

"I understand," she said, bobbing her head.

"I'm putting a man with you, one of Chief Anderson's rookies. You aren't to leave his side, you hear me?"

"Yes, okay."

Clay still looked doubtful. "Are you sure you don't want to go back to the cottage and wait with my mother and Ana?"

"And half the other wives and mothers in town? No, thanks. I can't take it, Clay. I can't take the pitying looks and the dread in their eyes. I can't take what they're all thinking." She pushed a hand through her hair. "I've paced, I've prayed, I've had too much tea and coffee, too many offers for pain pills and sedatives. I don't want a sedative. I need to be *out here,* looking for my son. Don't make me go back home."

"Okay, okay," he said, his hand touching her arm again. "As long as you do exactly as I say." At her nod, he continued. "Samson and I are going to track them on foot for as far as we can. We're going to search around the lighthouse. We think Hayes might have Ryan in there, maybe."

"The lighthouse?" Freddie's hand went to her throat. "Ryan's…he's fascinated with that place. He's been begging me to take him up inside it, but I never took the time. Do you think—"

Clay's expression was grim, a darkness surrounding his eyes. "I think Hayes is a desperate man and that he might try anything at this point. But if he's still on the island, we have a good chance of ending this tonight."

One way or another. Freddie saw that statement in the silent message from his eyes.

She heard him call out to Samson. The dog came running, eager to get to work. After all those weeks of training and rehabilitation, it had come down to this. Samson was a good dog, but was he up to this much intensity so soon after his recovery? Freddie prayed he was. *Help him, Lord. Help this dog find my son. Please, God, let them find my son.*

"Samson has the scent from the car, and I think he's going to be very aggressive when it comes to tracking Hayes," Clay told her. "We're about to get started."

He looked confident, sure, in control. Freddie lacked all three of those qualities right now. She felt weighed down with a dreadful fear, unsure of what to do or say, and she felt as if she were spiraling out of control in a dark, scary dream. But she'd do anything to get her son back, anything. Even if it meant having to give up Clay for the rest of her life.

She watched from inside Clay's truck, an officer beside her at the wheel, while Clay and Samson started heading back up the street toward the main road through town. Clay had Samson on a long leash attached to a tracking harness, but the dog took off so fast, Clay had to run to keep up with him.

"Here we go, ma'am," the young officer said. "If that dog gets too excited, Clay will let him loose." He was wearing a yellow polo shirt and long black shorts, the standard uniform of the island patrol. He didn't look a day over twenty. But he brought Freddie a small measure of comfort, at least. In spite of that, her skin crawled with unhinged nerves and her guilt crashed and bashed against her insides like a great raging wave. She looked up the street toward Clay and told herself to stay calm so he wouldn't send her back to just sit and wait at home.

"Thank you," she said to the patrol officer, her hand gripping the door of the truck as they crept along. She looked out the window, her eyes chasing each shadow, each movement, as she searched in the dark for her little lost boy.

They had to be in the lighthouse.

Samson had alerted almost immediately, straining at his harness, his nose lifting in the air toward the tall, bright red-and-white structure that sat on a jutting piece of shore at the uppermost tip of the island. Off in the distance to the west, Clay could just make out the silhouette of Hidden Hill, his brother's fancy mansion-turned-hotel. Since it was closed right now for renovations, other than construction workers, Clay was probably the only person on the island who'd used the great house this summer.

He had to wonder now if Todd Hayes had been watching him the whole time. If so, that would mean the other man knew not only Clay's schedule, but Freddie and Ryan's, too. He would have seen them at the house together, swimming in the pool, hanging out in the back gardens as they put Samson through his paces. He would have watched and waited for just the right moment.

And he would have known almost to the day and hour when Clay had left Sunset Island.

Clay silently berated himself for being so careless and stupid. But then, he'd left the island mad and hurt because Freddie didn't want him around. Now he wished he could take back his pride and his anger. He wished he'd made sure she and Ryan were safe before he'd headed back to Atlanta.

"What do you want to do?" Chief Anderson asked in a tight whisper. "I can surround the lighthouse with men, but I don't want to spook him. Not if he's got that kid in there."

Clay knew what he had to do. "I'm going in," he told the chief. "Alone."

"What about your dog? He'd nab the suspect in a minute."

Clay watched Samson pacing on a cluster of rocks. "I'm not sending Samson in just yet. He's tired and hungry and he's still recovering from a hip fracture. I don't want to put him in danger, but even more important, I don't want to endanger the child. Samson could get very aggressive in there and Ryan might get bitten by accident." He glanced back at the truck where Freddie sat from a distance, watching. Then he repeated his plan. "So…I'm going in alone."

"That don't sound like a good idea, son," Chief Anderson replied, his head moving against his thick neck. "Take some backup—human backup—at least."

"I can do it," Clay responded. "The element of surprise."

"I don't like surprises," Chief Anderson said, his expression stubborn. "I don't like it one bit."

"We have to see if they're even in there," Clay said. "Samson seems to think somebody is in that lighthouse."

"Then let Samson go in."

"Right. So Hayes can shoot him, or hurt Ryan? That won't help the situation."

"It won't help nobody if you get yourself shot up, either," the Chief reasoned. "Just let me put a couple of men on you, at least."

Clay thought about that for a minute. "Okay. Surround the perimeter of the lighthouse with armed men. I'm going in. Let one of your men follow me at a distance—we don't need two people getting shot at. When I get to that window about halfway up, I'll radio if I find anything, okay?"

"I don't like it."

"Chief, let me handle this," Clay retorted. "Just listen and let me do my job."

Chief Anderson stared him down for a full minute. "Well, I reckon you know more about this kind of procedure than we do. We don't get much of this kind of stuff around here."

"Exactly," Clay said, nodding. "I think I can handle it."

At least he hoped he could. Last time he'd been in a situation such as this, both he and Samson had wound up injured and the suspect had ended up dead. As much as he felt loathing toward Todd Hayes, he didn't want to kill the man right in front of Ryan. But then, he had to do something.

"Don't go being a hero now," the chief warned, as if he could read Clay's thoughts. "Make sure your radio is on and working."

"I don't intend to do anything stupid," Clay replied, his gun already out of its holster. "I just want to get that little boy back to his mother." He checked his radio, then turned toward Samson. "Stay."

The dog whimpered in protest, but he sat down on the planked pier leading toward the lighthouse. The chief waved his men forward, then gave them the signal to stand down until they got some sort of sign from Clay.

Clay treaded toward the dark lighthouse, wondering if he'd find anything inside. Wondering if he was too late.

"I can't just sit here," Freddie told Officer Stanley. "I have to do something."

"No, ma'am," the young man said, his dark eyes going wide. "I have strict orders to keep you out of harm's way."

"My son *is* in harm's way," Freddie countered, already opening the truck door.

Officer Stanley was out of the truck and around the

front before she could even think of getting closer to the deserted lighthouse. "Ma'am, if you want to help your boy, you need to stay here with me. If you alarm the suspect, he could do something very dangerous."

Freddie's nerves ripped apart like a shredded flap of sail, but she saw the wisdom of the man's suggestion. "All right," she said, her eyes on the lighthouse. When she saw a lone figure moving silently toward the door, she breathed a sigh of relief. Clay was going in there. For Ryan. For her. Then a new fear clawed its way up her spine.

What if something happened to Clay?

"Oh, no," she said, bringing a hand to her mouth. "I can't lose both of them, Lord. Not this way."

Officer Stanley gave her a keen look. "Go ahead and pray, ma'am. That's a good idea."

Freddie wanted to laugh out loud. "Do you really think my prayers will help?"

"Couldn't hurt," the young man said, his expression a cross between doubt for her sanity and fear that she'd try to run from him. "My mama always says when we've lost everything else, we still have prayer."

Freddie couldn't argue with that. "Okay…I'll pray. I've been praying. I just don't know if I deserve God's help."

Officer Stanley glanced at the lighthouse, then back to her. "God understands we're only human, ma'am. I think He's willing to listen at least." He lowered his head. "I mean, that's a little boy in there."

Freddie felt a great lump forming in her throat. So

many people were trying to help her and Ryan. This island was like a little family, a clan where everyone watched out for everyone else. If only someone had been able to help Ryan and Lee this afternoon.

She didn't know how to respond to so much kindness. It had been so long since she'd had kindness in her life. Maybe if she'd resisted less and opened up her heart more, none of this would have happened. Maybe more people would have been aware of Todd and his threats, if she'd only told them and asked them for help. Now, she could only hope that God would protect her son, so she could make it up to Ryan.

And to Clay, somehow. She might not be able to have a life with Clay, but she could at least be a little more kind to him. He'd gone beyond the duty of friendship to come back here and help her.

She owed him her kindness and her gratitude, and so much more. She looked toward the lighthouse, hoping against hope that her son would be found alive and well. And she prayed, not only for Ryan, but for the man who'd taken him.

And especially for the man who was trying to rescue him.

Clay was sweating. Inch by inch, he'd made his way up the newly remodeled spiral oak staircase in the lighthouse. The newly painted door to the attached living quarters had been pried open, but the tall cone-shape building was still and silent, its welcoming beam turned off due to the continuing renovations. Except for the occasional flow of moonlight through the clouds, the place was pitch-dark, and so far, he'd heard no sounds of life.

Which had him on edge all the way to his bones. What if—

He couldn't think of finding Ryan hurt or dead. He refused to think in those terms. The boy had to be all right. Surely his uncle wouldn't do him any harm. But then, from what Freddie had told him, Todd Hayes was a very volatile, dangerous man. And now he was desperate, too.

Not a good combination.

Clay was now at the first window. He couldn't give a hand signal in the dark, but there was nothing much to report so far, anyway. After whispering his location and status into the mouthpiece at his shoulder, he motioned to the officer tailing him at the bottom of the stairs, then went past the window and carefully moved up the winding stairs toward the top of the round house. He'd just made it around the uppermost spiral when a board creaked underneath his feet. He stopped, his weapon ready, his body on full alert. He held his breath, sweat pooling between his shoulder blades.

And then he heard it. A movement up above. Clay knew he had two choices—to hurry up the stairs and confront whoever was up there, or to signal for backup.

Remembering the last encounter he'd had with a dangerous criminal, Clay took a breath and counted to ten.

Don't be a hero. He had to get to Ryan, but he had to do it by the book so there would no mistakes, no cause for the law to set Todd Hayes free.

Clay turned toward the officer crouched about ten feet below him, his left arm moving back and forth in the signal that someone was indeed up in the lighthouse. Just to be sure, he whispered in the radio at his neck. After giving the code for more backup, Clay said, "I think he's up at the top. I'm going in."

Freddie saw the movement of several dark-clad men. They were heading toward the lighthouse. Then she saw Samson being held back by one of the officers. She also noticed that Samson's leash and harness were off. Just in case? The dog didn't bark, but Freddie could tell Samson wanted to go into the open building. She knew how the canine felt. If she could, she'd run all the way to the top and confront Todd.

But that might harm her son and Clay.

"Why didn't he take Samson with him?" she said, not realizing she'd voiced the question out loud until Officer Stanley turned to stare at her.

"He's worried about the K-9, ma'am. Samson's been tracking well into the night. And he's still recovering from an injury. Clay probably thought Samson wouldn't be at his best, or that he might accidentally bite the child in all the ruckus."

As far as Samson biting Ryan by accident, Freddie didn't think Samson would make that kind of mistake. "Samson wouldn't hurt Ryan." The dog would go right for Todd Hayes, she was sure. But then, she couldn't be sure what *Todd* would do. She glanced back toward the lighthouse, thinking of Clay. "So he'll risk his life, but not his partner's?"

Freddie didn't wait for an answer. She couldn't let Clay do this. He should have taken Samson with him. And from the way the dog was growling and pacing, Samson felt the same way.

She made a move toward the house, Officer Stanley right behind her. "Stand back, ma'am," he said, his voice raspy with excitement.

"I'm not going in there," she assured him, the words hollow and full of fear. "I just need to see what's happening."

"Clay radioed for backup," the officer told her. "That means he's found something."

And that could mean soon her son would be safe in her arms, Freddie thought. She hoped. She prayed. She closed her eyes for a split second. And then she heard gunshots.

Clay felt a bullet whizz by his head even as he ducked down. Moving back down the stairs, he took a breath as silence followed the two rapidly fired shots, then shouted into the radio. "Hold your fire. I repeat, stand by and hold your fire."

He got a garbled answer from Chief Anderson. "Ten-four. Are you injured?"

"Negative," Clay responded. "I'm okay. I'm going to try and make contact with suspect."

So Hayes was holed up inside here, but where was Ryan?

Deciding to test the waters, Clay called out. "Hayes, we've got you surrounded. Make this easy on yourself and the boy. Come on out with your hands up."

"I ain't coming out," came the ragged reply. "I'm not going anywhere without my nephew."

"Do you have the boy with you?"

"Why don't you come on up and see for yourself?"

Clay knew what that meant. Hayes would kill him on the spot. "Let Ryan talk to me." Silence. Clay shouted, calling out to Ryan. "Ryan, are you in there?"

"Why don't you shut up and get lost!" Hayes answered back.

Clay hit his hand on the staircase. "Listen, Hayes, a lot of people care about that little boy. Just bring Ryan out and maybe we can negotiate."

"Yeah, right. I'm done with negotiating. I tried to be reasonable, but Freddie didn't want to let me see my own kin. We're doing things my way now."

Clay stayed still. This was now going from a kidnapping to a hostage situation. And he didn't have the backup or the experience to handle this. "What do you want, Hayes?"

"I want safe passage off this island," came the heated reply. "With my nephew."

Clay knew enough to try to give the right answers. "I'll have to see what I can do. First, let me talk to Ryan, just so I can tell his mother he's safe."

There was a long silence, then another shout. "No deal. You tell those men to stand down right now, to back up and move away, or…or something's gonna happen that we'll all regret."

"You don't want to harm the boy, Hayes," Clay shouted, hoping Chief Anderson was getting all of this. "Don't harm the boy. We'll talk. We'll find a way to end this without anyone getting hurt."

"I'm not going to jail—not for only wanting to see my nephew," Hayes screamed. "I'm telling you to back off, or you'll all regret it." Just to emphasize his point, Hayes fired another round of gunshots.

Freddie's nerves jumped with each shot fired. She'd seen the men rushing forward, but now they were all crouched down and waiting. "What are they doing?" she asked Officer Stanley, impatience and fear causing her to rush forward.

"Following orders," the officer responded, one strong hand on her arm. "Clay must be communicating with them. He's probably trying to talk down the suspect."

"Didn't you hear that gunfire? Todd Hayes can't be talked down," she retorted, her pacing wearing a hole in the muddy, rutted road. "They need to go in there and get my son."

Officer Stanley turned to face her, a look of compassion on his face. "Ma'am—"

"My name is Freddie," she said, the words harsh and clipped.

"Freddie, Clay Dempsey knows what he's doing, I'm sure. He deals with this kind of thing up in Atlanta. You just hang on and stay calm."

"I can't stay calm," Freddie said, pushing at her hair as she paced. "I can't stay calm when that man has my child in there. Somebody better do something soon, or I'll go into that lighthouse myself."

She saw Samson then. The dog hovered and growled, his ears perked up, his whole stance alerted toward the open door of the lighthouse. Samson knew something was wrong, just as Freddie knew it. And Samson would do whatever it took to protect his partner and her son.

Tears welled in Freddie's eyes, but she told herself she didn't have a choice. Freddie knew the command from helping Clay retrain Samson. She knew what she had to do.

Without stopping to think, she pushed past the surprised police officer standing with her and called out to Samson. "Samson, go find. Bite, Samson. Go find. Bite!"

Samson took off toward the lighthouse, his excited barks indicating that Freddie had read his mind. Freddie ran up to the rocks where the rest of the officers were still waiting.

Chief Anderson grabbed her by the arm, his angry shout lifting out into the night. "Woman, what have you gone and done?"

"I'm trying to save Clay and my son," Freddie screamed.

Chief Anderson just shook his head. "No, you probably just sentenced them both to death."

Freddie's gut told her she'd done the right thing. Samson was Clay's partner. Samson would know what to do.

After all, he'd been trained to search and rescue. He'd also been trained to attack anyone who appeared hostile and threatening.

Todd Hayes was hostile and threatening. And she prayed Samson was headed right for him.

Chapter Sixteen

Everything after that became a blur to Clay. He heard Samson barking, felt the whish of air and the brush of fur as the great dog cleared the stairs and hurled himself up into the landing. Clay shouted for backup, then followed Samson into the top of the structure. By the time Clay got there, the dog had Todd Hayes cornered outside up against the steel railing of the narrow wraparound balcony.

Samson had gone for Hayes's legs and now had the man by the right shin in a teeth-baring death grip. Clay could see the rage and dislike in Samson's eyes. The dog's instincts told him this man was trouble.

"Samson, heel!" Clay called, holding his gun on Hayes as he advanced out onto the balcony. The wind whipped around them, sending damp sprays of mist over Clay's sweat-soaked body. Below the waves crashed and hissed, their anger every bit as sharp and piercing as Samson's teeth. Samson didn't want to let go.

"Samson, back!" Clay shouted, his tone firm and loud.

Samson stood back, his growls and snarls indicating he was more than ready for another go at it.

"I'm going to kill your dog," Hayes said through huffs of breath, the pain in his face causing him to look demented.

"I wouldn't try that," Clay retorted, his gun aimed for Hayes's good leg. "You're injured, Hayes. The game is up. Now tell me where Ryan is."

Todd Hayes grinned in spite of his pain. He was a big, muscular man, but Clay could see the jagged fatigue surrounding the dark, sunken skin around his eyes.

And Clay could see that this man wasn't about to give up so easily. In the next second, Hayes lifted his hidden weapon toward Clay at about the same time Samson, sensing danger, lunged for him again.

Clay fired back purely by instinct, but missed. Hayes ducked away from Samson's attack and Clay's bullet, then whirled, his gun aimed right at Clay. It all happened in a split second. Samson leaped back toward Hayes just as the shot sounded out into the night. A sense of déjà vu overcame Clay as he heard Samson whimper then fall. Clay watched as his partner slumped over against the thin iron of the railing, watched as Samson seemed to go to sleep right in front of his eyes.

"Told you I was gonna kill him," Todd Hayes said, his gun by his side now, his demeanor completely calm.

Clay advanced, his gun pointed at Hayes's face. "I could kill *you,*" he said, the words gritty and full of loathing. "But then, that would make me too much *like* you. And I am nothing like you, Hayes."

"Oh, yeah. You so sure about that, cop?"

"Very sure." Clay didn't care if the other man had a gun. He advanced and yanked Hayes by the right arm, his weapon steady in spite of the rapid beating inside his chest. "Drop it."

Hayes did as he was told, still smiling. "I don't mind so much now. Ryan's good and gone. You'll never find him."

"What are you saying?" Clay asked, his eyes darting to his partner. Samson didn't move. Clay refused to think about that now. "Where's the boy, Hayes?"

"A long way from here," Hayes replied.

Clay's backup came then. The place was suddenly swarming with armed men.

And one crying, screaming, angry woman.

"Where's my son?" Freddie said, relief at seeing Clay alive giving her a new surge of energy that only boosted her anger and wrath. She lurched toward Hayes before anyone could stop her, grabbing him by his sweat-soaked T-shirt, the hate and hurt in her heart making her want to smack him. "What have you done with my son?"

Hayes smiled even while he was being handcuffed. It was a sickening smile, a look that made Freddie want to throw up. "He's with his grandmother. And they're probably halfway back to Texas by now. They could even be in Mexico. I told Ryan he'd like Mexico."

"Pearl? Pearl was in on this with you!"

"All the way," Hayes said. "She loves that boy. And she'll do anything I ask her to do."

"No, no," Freddie said, her fists pounding into the man's chest. "How could you do this? How could you do this to my little boy?"

"He needed to be with family," Hayes retorted with a smug look. "And now, he will be. You'll never find him."

Freddie decided right then that there truly was evil in this world. She was staring it in the face. But she refused to back down. "You have to tell me where he is, Todd. I'm his mother."

"He belongs with his *real* family," Todd Hayes hissed. "And that means you don't have any say in the matter."

"Yes, we do," Clay said, yanking Hayes around so they could take him down the stairs and on to jail. "We have a say in the matter, because you broke the law, Hayes, and because Freddie is Ryan's mother. You're under arrest for kidnapping, child endangerment, assault and battery, and I'm sure I'll think of a few more." Then he read Todd Hayes his rights.

"I know my rights," Hayes shouted. "I need a doctor for this leg. I'm bleeding to death." He kept hollering all the way down the stairs. "I'm not worried. I have connections. I'll be out and with Ryan before you know it, Miss Uppity. You and your cop boyfriend have made a serious mistake, messing with me and mine. You'll never see your son again."

Freddie turned to face Clay, tears streaming down her face. "He can't mean that. He can't—"

Then she stopped, her nightmares turning from frightened to anguished as she looked down. "Oh, Samson. Samson?"

She fell beside the still animal, tears falling down her face as all the turmoil inside her hit with the force of a tidal wave. "Samson, I'm so sorry. Samson, wake up, boy. Please, wake up."

Clay bent down beside her, then lifted Samson's head. "Is he dead?"

Freddie felt around on a spot behind Samson's left front leg, then once again along his back leg, sobs causing her whole body to shake. "He has a pulse, but he's losing so much blood. I don't know if I can—"

Clay went on his knees and took her by her arms. "Freddie, listen to me. You save my dog, do you hear me?"

She nodded, the movement slow and shell-shocked.

Clay's eyes were shining with tears. "Freddie, I'm going to find Ryan. I will find him and bring him home. But you have to try and save Samson. Freddie, please, for me?"

"Oh, Clay." She reached up to touch the tears streaming down his face. "I shouldn't have sent him in here, but you needed him. You needed your partner."

"You did the right thing," Clay said, his voice raspy, his eyes filled with pain and regret. "He should have been with me." Then he pushed her hand away. "I have to finish my job. Get Samson to the clinic," he said, "before it's too late."

Freddie nodded again, his heart-wrenching plea pushing through her shock. Clay Dempsey was one of the bravest men she'd ever known. She had to be brave for him. Because of him. "Okay. Okay. Find Pearl. She wouldn't hurt Ryan, but…she can't take him away. He belongs with me."

"I will," Clay promised. "I will."

He touched a hand to Samson's nose. "You hang in there, buddy, you hear me? We've come too far—you can't leave us now, Samson. You can't die on me, buddy."

He got up, wiped his face, then turned and headed down the stairs.

"I came to help."

Freddie looked up from the surgery to find Lee Fletcher standing at the door of the operating room. Her eyes held his for a long while, then she nodded. "I could use some help."

Kate was already there. "Give me that gauze, Kate," Freddie said, her shoulders aching with fatigue, her mind numb with worry and shock.

Lee came close, all scrubbed up and ready to work. "Took a bullet, did you, old fellow?"

"It's bad," Kate said. "He's lost a lot of blood." She glanced up at the fluids going into Samson's still body. "Doc says we don't have the right equipment—"

"I had to do emergency surgery," Freddie said, finishing Kate's sentence. "We don't have time to get him to Savannah."

"Can you find the bullet, Doc?" Lee asked as he went about the routine tasks involved in operating on an animal.

"I think I have it."

Freddie was thankful for the routine, thankful for the silent calm of her clinic. Flashes of the nightmare she was living kept pushing at her consciousness. She remembered wrapping Samson in a blanket the paramedics had given her after they'd applied a tourniquet to stop the bleeding. She remembered Officer Stanley lifting the lifeless animal and hurriedly carrying him down the winding stairs, the other officers holding their hats at their hearts in honor of a fallen colleague.

She remembered, but now she couldn't make her mind move past saving Samson. If she gave in to the terror, she'd lose focus and go mad with worry about Clay and her son.

"It punctured a lung and now it's lodged underneath his left rib cage. But it missed his heart, thank goodness.

If we can get it out and get him sewn back up, he might make it through the night."

"It's almost dawn," Lee pointed out, his head still bandaged. "What a night."

Freddie glanced up at him, her heart piercing with gratitude. "I didn't thank you, Lee. For trying to help Ryan."

Lee glanced up, then looked back down at Samson. "Ah, now, I just did what anybody woulda done, Doc. I couldn't let that little boy go off with that idiot."

That brought a quick, tired smile to Freddie's face. "No, you couldn't do that. I appreciate what you did, Lee. And I will never doubt you again."

"Let's just get this here doggy well for Clay," Lee responded in a gruff manner.

"Good idea."

Freddie went back to her work. She had to save Samson. For Clay's sake.

While she worked on the dog, she prayed that Clay had found out where Pearl had taken Ryan. Her son was out there somewhere, scared and confused. And now, Clay was out there on his own, trying to find him.

Keep them safe, Lord.

He was on his own now. He didn't have Samson to guide him. Clay felt the emptiness of that realization down to his very bones. It felt odd, being out on the hunt without his sidekick. He'd always depended on Samson to get him through any situation.

Samson had once again saved Clay's life.

Now Clay had to save a little boy.

He needed help from a higher source; he needed to turn to God. "You hear me, Lord? Could You please just send me a little reinforcement? It's been a long night, and I'm really tired."

So tired. He'd driven every inch of this island. They'd put out an all points bulletin on Pearl Hayes, believing she might still be on the island since they'd had no reports of stolen or missing vehicles, and nothing from the roadblocks, or even the nearby airports and bus terminals. But if she'd taken the boy back to Texas—

Texas bordered Mexico. Todd Hayes had hinted in interrogation that his mother might try to take Ryan out of the country. If she took that boy into Mexico, it might be a long time before they ever found Ryan. If they ever did.

Clay could only hope that Pearl Hayes would have the good sense to think about her actions. Especially now that it had been blasted all over the local and national news about the kidnapping and Todd Hayes's arrest.

A mother wouldn't leave her son.

Even if that son was evil and dangerous.

Clay was hoping that would keep Pearl on the island. With Ryan.

Other than that speculation, he had very little to go

on. But everyone was watching and looking. At least he had help in that way. He could depend on the islanders to watch and pray. It was his last hope.

The call came around 6:00 a.m.

"Clay? Clay Dempsey? Is that you?"

Clay strained to hear the feeble voice on the other end of the cell phone. "Miss McPherson?"

"I think I saw that woman. The one y'all been looking for. Got your number from Rock."

Clay sat up straight against the seat of his truck. "Where? Where, Miss Milly?"

"Down at the motel. You know, that old motel by the boardwalk."

"The Sunset Beachside?" Clay asked, wondering how Milly McPherson had managed to even see anything with her cataracts.

"That's the one, son. I was out for my morning walk 'bout an hour ago, and lo and behold, I saw a woman kind of suspicious and sneaky near a room. She was tapping on the door, then looking around. Finally, a little boy came to the door, looking all sleepy-eyed. She musta got them breakfast. I recognized the take-out bag from Two Mikes."

"Are you sure?" Clay asked, excited but full of dread at the same time. He couldn't take another letdown. "Are you sure she had Ryan with her?"

"Of course I'm sure," came the firm reply. "The boy

ran out the door when she unlocked it. He waved to me and called me by name. That is, before that old woman yanked him by the shirt and rushed him inside that room. Apparently, she'd left him there alone while she went for breakfast. That was a dumb thing to do, if you ask me."

Clay thanked the heavens for dumb moves.

"I'm on my way," Clay said, already putting the truck in reverse as he also thanked the good Lord for sharp-as-a-tack Milly McPherson. He called Chief Anderson. "I think we found them." The chief said he'd meet Clay at the Beachside.

"Thank You, God," Clay said, hitting his hand on the steering wheel. "Maybe, just maybe, this day will end on a good note, after all."

Chapter Seventeen

It only took a knock on the door and a shout of "Police, open up!" for Pearl Hayes to let them in.

"I didn't want it to happen like this," she said as she ushered Clay and Chief Anderson into the sparse room. "Todd said we were just coming for a visit. I didn't know he was gonna take the boy. He told me to wait here with Ryan. Said he had to find a car or another way off this island."

Clay looked at the frail, aged woman standing with tears running down her withered face. Pearl Hayes looked hardened and haggard, her gray-streaked curly hair matted against her face as if she hadn't bothered to comb it, her eyes red-rimmed and darting.

"Where's my Todd?" she asked as Clay went to the bed where Ryan was sleeping peacefully. "We were in the lighthouse, but he made me sneak Ryan out when it got dark enough. Told us to come back to the room. He was supposed to come and get us at dawn."

"So all that talk about Mexico, that was just a bluff?"

Pearl's aged face shook with pulsing veins. "Mexico? I don't know what you're talking about. Where's my son?"

"Todd's in jail," Clay told the woman. Then because he was tired and relieved, he turned to Pearl and tried to be gentle. "Mrs. Hayes, we need you to cooperate with us. It might help you."

"Will it help Todd?"

"I don't know about that," Clay said, trying to be honest with the distraught woman. "Todd kidnapped Ryan and tried to smuggle him off the island. That's a serious crime. He's also being charged with assault and battery. Your son is in a lot of trouble."

"I need to call my husband," Pearl said, wiping her eyes with a wadded-up tissue.

"You can do that down at the station," the chief told her. "We have to take you in, ma'am."

"I understand," Pearl said. "I want to see my son and call my husband. They'll know what to do."

Clay nodded, not wanting to get in a squabble with a woman who was clearly near the end of her rope. "I have to take Ryan to his mother now," he told Pearl in a low voice.

Pearl started crying all over again. "I'll get him ready."

She went over to Ryan and gently touched a shaking hand on his arm. "Ryan, honey, wake up now.

Grandma has to go, sugar. And…you need to go home to your mama."

Ryan stirred, wiped a hand over his eyes, then sat up, fear and confusion marring his face until he saw Clay. "Clay!" he said, hurling himself into Clay's arms.

Clay took the boy and held him close as Ryan balanced his bare feet on the lumpy bed. "Hey, buddy. Ready to go see your mother?"

"Yes, sir," Ryan said. "I was so scared. Uncle Todd was mad at me…and he hurt Lee."

"I know, buddy. It's all right now. Lee's just fine and…Uncle Todd isn't mad at you, not at all."

"Where is he then?" Ryan asked, his big eyes full of innocence and questions. "Why'd he make us hide in this room?"

Pearl touched a hand to Ryan's arm. "He had to get back to work, honey. And I have to go with this nice man here, to see your uncle." She swallowed, pushed a hand through her hair. "Can Grandma have a big hug? I might…it might be a while before I can see you again."

Ryan looked at Clay. Clay nodded, then watched the boy and his grandmother hugging goodbye. He hated this for Pearl. She was probably just as innocent in all of this as Ryan was. She'd been manipulated by her bully of a son for too long to understand the consequences of what she'd been forced to do. While his heart went out to Pearl Hayes, he also felt the urgency of getting Ryan back to Freddie.

"We have to go now, Mrs. Hayes," he said.

Pearl let go of Ryan, then turned to face the chief. "I'm ready."

Clay took Ryan back in his arms. Ryan lifted his head, looking around. "Where's Samson?"

Clay felt a lump forming in his throat. "He's…he's with your mom. Let's go see them, okay?"

"We'll have to wait and see," Freddie told Ana and Rock an hour after she'd finished surgery on Samson. They were all sitting in the waiting area of the clinic. "I did what I could for him. We got the bullet out and we've managed to stabilize his damaged lung. The rest is—"

Just then, the door burst open and Ryan rushed in. "Mom?"

Freddie's hand went to her mouth as she fell onto her knees. "Ryan?"

The boy bounded into her arms, hugging her as he laid his head on her shoulder. "Mom, I'm sorry we scared you. Uncle Todd told me it was okay. He said we'd go on a big adventure and you wouldn't mind. Lee tried to tell me to come check with you first, but I was so glad to see Uncle Todd, I kinda forgot the rules."

"It's okay, baby. It's okay. You're here now. You're safe." She glanced over Ryan's head to Clay, mouthing a silent "thank you" to the man who'd found her child. "Are you all right?" she asked Ryan as she sank down onto the nearest bench with him still in her lap. "Let me get a look at you."

"Aw, Mom, I'm fine. But I sure want to sleep in my own bed again. Staying in the lighthouse was fun at first, but then I got scared. And that motel bed was bumpy."

Freddie laughed, wiping tears away. "And I want you to be back in your own bed. After you've rested, we'll have a long talk…about everything."

"Okay." Ryan looked around. "Where's Samson?"

Freddie's eyes locked with Clay's. She could see the same question in his grim expression. "Samson had an accident, honey. He's very sick. I had to help him."

"He'll be okay," Ryan said, bobbing his head. "You're the best animal doctor in the world."

Freddie kissed the top of her son's head. "I hope you're right. I tried my best." She was still looking at Clay, hoping he'd understand that she did try to save Samson.

"I want to see him," Clay said, pushing off the door-frame. "Where is he?"

"Room three," Freddie said, her arms still clinging to her son. The warmth of his little body brought her such a comfort, such an all-consuming relief that she had to swallow back tears again. She couldn't let him go.

"Mom, can I see Samson, too?"

She finally looked down at Ryan, then shot a frantic gaze toward Rock and Ana. Rock nodded, then said, "Samson might like a visit from his best friend."

"That's a good idea," Freddie said, realizing that if anyone could bring Samson back, it would be Ryan. "But you have to be very gentle and you need to talk to him in a quiet, inside voice, okay?"

"Okay," Ryan said, squirming out of Freddie's arms.

Clay was already in the room when she took Ryan in. Her heart bolted with lightning speed at seeing the man she loved bent over the still animal. She could tell Clay was fighting back tears. He looked so tired. His usually bright eyes were dark with fatigue and pain. His little-boy face looked as if it had aged overnight.

Ryan hurried to Clay's side, then took one of Samson's big paws in his little hand. "Samson, what's the matter, boy? Did you get a bad boo-boo?"

Clay looked down at the boy. "He…he was in the wrong place at the wrong time."

Freddie felt the condemnation of those words to her very soul. She wanted to tell Clay how sorry she was, but in her heart, she felt that if she hadn't sent Samson in to help his partner, Clay might be dead right now and her son might be thousands of miles away.

Ryan looked up at her, his face full of hope. "Is he going to live, Mommy?"

"I don't know," she said, too tired to be anything but honest. "We stopped the bleeding and…tried to fix his lung. He's a big, strong dog, so I'm praying that he'll make it through."

Clay turned then, his eyes clear and focused as he

stared at her. Clear and focused and devoid of any of the warm, familiar intensity she'd come to know and love. "Thank you for helping him."

He left the room. Freddie heard the clinic door slamming.

It was as if he'd slammed something hard and unyielding against her heart. Suddenly, all her fears and worries seemed to fall apart right before her eyes. She'd wanted to blame Clay—or rather her feelings for Clay—for her stupid actions yesterday, but none of this was Clay's fault. The joy of accepting that she loved him seemed to fill her heart once again, replacing all the doom and gloom she'd lived through since yesterday.

But she'd promised God so many things in her darkest hours. What should she do now?

She stood in the corner of the little examining room, watching her son talk softly to Samson. Then she looked up to find Rock watching her from the open door.

"Hi," he said.

Freddie couldn't speak, so she managed a nod.

"Ana and I can stay here with Samson and Ryan, if you need to get some air."

His unspoken message hung in the room between them. *Go to Clay. He needs you.*

"I'm afraid to leave them," she admitted, biting her lip to keep from crying out in rage and frustration.

"Ryan is safe now," Rock said. "Ana and I are right here. And Lee and Kate are nearby." He inclined his head toward the door. "He went out to the bay. It's within calling distance."

She pushed at her braid, then touched a hand to Ryan's hair. "Honey, I'm going to talk to Clay. I'll be just outside. Are you sure you're okay?"

Ryan looked up at her, saw the tears on her face. "I'm all right, Mommy. I was scared some with Uncle Todd, but he didn't hurt me. He mostly just wanted to talk. He took me to the lighthouse, but then Grandma Pearl came and took me to the hotel. I was just worried about Lee."

"Lee's just fine," Rock told the boy.

Ryan absorbed that, then glanced back at Freddie. "I can stay with Samson if you need to give Clay a hug."

Freddie's tears came full force then. "I do. I do need to hug Clay, to thank him for finding you. I'll be back in a minute."

"Okay," Ryan said as he turned back to Samson, his grubby hand stroking the dog's plush fur.

Freddie turned to hurry from the room, but she stopped as she brushed past Rock. "Last night…I made a bargain with God—"

Rock smiled, then bent his head. "You promised God that if He'd just bring your son back, you'd give up everything, right?"

"Right. Even Clay."

Rock touched a hand to her arm. "Freddie, God doesn't deal in bargains. God is all about love and forgiveness. Do you think He expects you to live up to that desperate bargain?"

"I don't want to do anything else to hurt my son."

"You'd hurt Ryan more if you turn away from the love Clay has to offer you."

"And what about God?"

"God will be right there with you. And Ryan's life will be all the better because of it. The only promise you need to make to God is the promise of your service and your faith. Christ died for us, so that we could live through Him. Go out and start doing that."

She lowered her head, then looked back at her son. "I have to go and talk to Clay."

"Go," Rock said. "We'll be right here."

She found him out on the dock, near some of the fancy yachts by the parasailing boats. He was sitting there watching the water lapping at the pilings, his head down, his hands clutching the splintered wood.

Freddie sat down beside him, then placed her hand over his. At first, his fingers felt stiff and cold against her touch, but she kept holding on until he gave up and clasped her hand in a tight gentleness.

"Is he dead?" His question was husky and hollow.

"No." She took his hand and held it even tighter. "No. Ryan is with him. He's talking to him and petting him. Rock and Ana are with them."

He lifted his head to stare out at the bay. The midmorning sun poured out over them like a beckoning light, warm and pure and full of radiance. "What a beautiful day," he said.

"After such a horrible night." She didn't know where to begin, so she just blurted it out. "Clay, I was wrong to send you away."

"I was wrong to expect you to want me in your life."

"But I do…want you in my life. Even though I promised God—"

He brought his head around then, his blue-green eyes capturing hers with a pure, honest look. "You promised God you'd give me up, in return for your son."

"Yes, but—"

He chuckled then, surprising her. "I made the same promise. I wanted to find Ryan and I was willing to do whatever needed to be done to get him back. Even if that meant losing you."

Freddie felt the humility of his sacrifice like a piercing shard through her heart, a beautiful pain that sealed her love for him completely as the shard turned back onto itself and healed her, at last.

Clay looked down at their joined hands. "So…I guess we can't be together after all."

"Rock says God doesn't expect us to bargain with Him. Rock says—"

"My brother says a lot of things. That doesn't make it right."

"What would make it right between us?"

He turned to her then, pulling his hand away from hers. At first, she thought he was going to leave her sitting there. But instead, he put his hands on her face and lifted her chin. "I guess the only way to prove to God that we can be faithful is to…love each other."

"Love each other?"

"Yeah, you know, like getting married and taking care of Ryan and always, always putting God first to make up for bargaining with Him." He held her face between his big, strong hands, the warmth of his tender touch making Freddie see that she had indeed been blessed by coming to Sunset Island.

"You and me?" she asked, awestruck.

"If you want me."

"I do," she said as she gazed up at him. "But I thought you were…I thought you hated me because of Samson—"

"Shh," he said, bringing his mouth to hers. "Don't even think that. It's okay. We each did what we had to do to get through this, Freddie. And now, I have so much more in my life. I'll miss Samson if he doesn't make it, but I have you and Ryan and…we're going to be okay, because we love each other."

He kissed her then, his lips gentle and reassuring, just like the sunshine that had come after the rain-filled night.

And then Ryan came running across the grass toward them, his grin splitting his face with pure joy. "He woke up!" Ryan shouted, his hands in the air. "Samson woke up and looked at me, Mommy."

Clay and Freddie both released a breath. Then Clay kissed Freddie and jumped up to grab Ryan in a bear hug. "That's the best news, buddy." He held Ryan on his hip with one arm as he reached down to Freddie with his other hand.

"Let's go see Samson."

Together, they walked back up the hill from the bay, the water behind them shimmering with the beginnings of a new day. Above them, a lone seagull lifted out in the wind, silently flying toward home.

Epilogue

Thanksgiving

"We made the paper again."

Eloise Dempsey turned and smiled at her family. They were all gathered around the big mahogany table in the formal dining room, across from her kitchen. Cy and Neda had gone overboard with a huge turkey and all the trimmings, but it had been worth all the effort.

Eloise had her whole family with her for the holidays, for the first time since the boys were all still living at home. And she had her extended family here—Freddie's father, Wade, was standing beside his daughter, beaming with pride. There were a few other welcome guests at the celebration, too.

"What did Greta Epperson write this time, Mom?" Clay asked, grinning over at Freddie.

"Oh, she wrote about your dramatic rescue of our little Ryan," Eloise replied, careful to keep her voice down so the children wouldn't hear. The whole family had agreed to avoid saying anything unpleasant around Ryan, as the boy was still confused about what exactly had happened to him back in September. "But then, that was all over the paper when it happened. Dear Greta was gushing with praise for you, Clay, since you are now officially the new Assistant Chief for our island patrol. And…she mentioned your upcoming wedding, in great detail. She thinks it's the neatest thing, having a dog *and* a little boy for your ring bearers."

"Oh, great," Freddie said as she placed steaming hot rolls provided by their special guest, Milly McPherson, on the already full table. "I guess I can expect Greta to be there with her photographer again." She grinned over at Clay. "She won't be able to resist a Christmas wedding."

Stone slapped his brother on the back. "That's right. Y'all met at our wedding, didn't you?"

"Sure did," Clay said. "Samson found her first, but I get to keep her."

Down the way, Miss McPherson huffed and slapped the table. "Boy always did go for what he wanted out of life." Then she smiled sweetly. "Glad to have you home for good, though, Clay."

Rock and Ana laughed and cuddled as everyone entered the room for grace. Rock took his wife's hand, then waited for the rest of the clan to grab a nearby hand. "I can't believe we're all here together, Mother. And that you somehow managed to get all three of us married off in one long, interesting summer." He glanced over at his wife. "And since we're all here, Ana and I have an announcement to make—"

"Oh, when is it due?" Eloise said, clasping her hands together.

Rock rolled his eyes, grinned. "Okay, Mother, okay. In about seven months. Yes, it's official. We're having a baby."

Ana beamed as Rock gave her a quick kiss. Everyone cheered and commented, until Eloise hit her tea glass with a knife to get their attention.

"Another prayer answered," Eloise said, taking Don Ashworth's hand, her love-struck grin shining through her proud tears. "I am so thankful for so many things this year. But mostly, I'm thankful for second chances."

"I agree," Stone said, winking at Tara, then grinning over at their three girls, Laurel, Amanda and MaryBeth.

Clay watched as Tara's girls and Don's son, Cal Ashworth—who'd once been Laurel's love interest but was now more like her older brother since she was "in love" with a star high school quarterback in Savannah—gathered in clear view at the smaller table in the kitchen, Ryan right beside them. "We've all been blessed," he said, his fingers squeezing Freddie's on one side and Ana's on the other.

Rock cleared his throat to say grace, but Ana's cell phone chimed.

"Oh, excuse me," Ana said, grabbing for her nearby purse. She said a hasty hello, then started laughing. "Yes, Jackie, everyone knows. Yes, I hear Tina and Charlotte cheering in the background. Yes, we're all thrilled. Now will you please go back to your dinner with your families and let me do the same?" Then she got misty-eyed again. "Thanks. Tell Tina and Charlotte I love and appreciate them—and you."

Eloise gave Ana an understanding smile. "We are all so happy for you two."

Rock kissed his wife again, while Clay glanced at Freddie, a new hope centered in his heart.

Rock said grace, repeating their thanks for forgiveness, second chances and a baby on the way. Then he lifted his head and grinned. "Can we eat now, Mother? Please?"

"I guess we've kept you waiting long enough," Eloise replied jovially. "Everyone, find a seat. Don has agreed to carve the turkey."

Don Ashworth looked all hot and bothered as he held the carving knife out over the big bird. "Before I do that, I have a question for your mother here."

Everyone looked surprised, including Eloise. "What is it, Don? Did I forget to put something on the table?"

"No, I'm the one putting something on the table," Don said. "I'm putting out a proposal, and I'm asking your sons for their permission...to *officially* date you, Eloise. That is if...I mean, would you...like to go out with me?"

Stone glanced at his mother, his frown showing his surprise. "Mother, I didn't even know you and Mr. Ashworth were...uh...close."

"Can she answer the question before y'all start protesting?" Don said, his nervousness clear by the way the big knife was shaking in his unsteady hand. "Eloise?"

Eloise stood up to stare at the handsome gray-haired man across from her. "I...well...I'd be honored to *officially* date you, Don."

Rock shot Ana a look. "Did you know about this?"

"Sorta," Ana said, passing the mashed potatoes to an amused Tara. "I mean, they have dinner together at least once a week as it is."

"Did you?" Stone asked Tara, who was suddenly busy moving the rolls aside to make room for the peas.

"I might have heard something."

Clay looked over at Freddie. "I guess you probably knew about this, too, right?"

"I've been busy planning my wedding," Freddie said, her eyes on the cranberry sauce on her plate.

"Humph," Miss McPherson said, waving a hand in the air. "Well, get on with it, man. Are you going to court the woman or not?"

"Oh..." Don said, clearing his throat, "I guess Eloise and I are gonna start dating and seeing a lot more of each other. A whole lot, if I have my way. Anyone have a problem with that?"

They heard a loud bark, followed by a hissing sound.

Ryan jumped up to run into the big, open parlor across the way. "Uh-oh, Mommy. Samson just spotted BoBo. I think they're gonna—"

Before Ryan could get the words out, a shrieking meowing cat came running through the kitchen, followed by a big German shepherd dog.

"They're just playing," Amanda announced as she scooped up the scared cat. "Samson wouldn't hurt his best friend, would you now, Samson? Remember how BoBo played with you while you were getting better?"

"I don't think Samson will hurt BoBo," Freddie said, her eyes on the still-healing dog. "He can't get around as quickly these days, but he sure gives it a valiant effort."

"Samson, sit and mind your manners," Clay cautioned.

Samson stood at the open archway, sniffing the air, his big brown eyes moving from the scrawny cat to the fat, succulent bird sitting on the table. With a grunt and a wagging of his tail, he plopped down beside Clay, his expression telling everyone he'd rather wait for a nice turkey bone than fool with a silly old cat.

"I'm hungry," Rock repeated, a bit of a whine in his voice. "And I can't have pie until I eat my vegetables."

"Let's eat then," Clay said, passing the gravy.

Don carved the bird, one eye on Eloise. She leaned over and kissed him on the cheek.

"Oh, my stepgrandmother's going to date your Daddy," Laurel exclaimed to Cal, clearly appalled at this turn of events. "Mother—"

"That just means you'll have another grandfatherly figure in your life," Tara replied, laughing at her oldest daughter. "And Cal will be like your *unofficial* uncle."

"Uncle Cal," Laurel teased, poking Cal in the ribs.

"Great," Cal said, rolling his eyes.

"It'll be okay," Rock assured the teenager, grinning as he finally nabbed a turkey leg. "It's all going to be okay, in God's own time."

"I've sure missed this," Freddie's father, Wade, said.

"Missed what?" Stone asked as he buttered his roll.

"The sweet chaos of family," Wade Noble replied. Then he kissed his daughter. "Thanks for inviting me. And I'm with Rock. I can't wait for some of that sweet-potato pie."

Everyone laughed as the dishes continued making their way around the table. Samson barked his approval, then lowered his head onto the floor, his eyes still on that turkey.

"I love you," Clay told Freddie, holding her hand under the table, the feel of her diamond solitaire engagement ring warm and sure underneath his fingers. He'd given it to her at the turning point where the beach curved to meet the bay, one night after a long, romantic walk. They'd reached a new point in their lives now. And Clay could see their future stretching out like a distant vista, full of promise.

"I love you, too," Freddie replied, her smile radiant.

"Even though I'm a cop?"

"*Because* you're a cop," she replied.

* * * * *

Dear Reader,

I hope you enjoyed the last story of my SUNSET ISLAND series. I have to admit, I'm going to miss Rock, Stone, Clay and all the characters who took over my heart and my head while I was writing this series.

Clay was a gentle soul, molded and shaped by the things he saw and felt as a child who'd lost his father. Clay only wanted to please everyone else, but he had to learn that God wants us to find our own heart along the path of life, and sometimes we have to follow that course, in spite of what others might want for us instead. Clay found his heart again when he fell in love with Freddie. He was the potter's clay, but thanks to God's love and Freddie's change of heart, Clay also found the strength to shape his own life.

I hope this story gives you strength. Don't let past hurts and old wounds keep you away from God's love. Turn back to the Lord and let Him shape you and mold you with His tender touch. You can have a new beginning, just as Clay and Freddie did, and you, too, can become the Potter's clay.

Until next time, may the angels watch over you—always.

Lenora Worth